W9-ANR-526

UNIVERSAL PICTURES
and
EMI FILMS
present
ROBERT DE NIRO
in
"THE DEER HUNTER"
A MICHAEL CIMINO FILM
Co-starring
JOHN CAZALE · JOHN SAVAGE · MERYL STREEP · CHRISTOPHER WALKEN
Music by STANLEY MYERS Director of photography VILMOS ZSIGMOND A.S.C.
Executive Producers MICHAEL DEELEY and BARRY SPIKINGS
Produced by JOHN PEVERALL Story by MICHAEL CIMINO &
DERIC WASHBURN and LOUIS GARFINKLE & QUINN K. REDEKER
Screenplay by DERIC WASHBURN Directed by MICHAEL CIMINO
A UNIVERSAL RELEASE

THE DEER HUNTER

E.M. Corder

NEW YORK

First Exeter Books edition 1979

Exeter Books
Distributed by Bookthrift, Inc.
New York, New York

ISBN 0-89673-035-2

Library of Congress Number 79-53098

There is no hunting like the hunting of man, and those who have hunted armed men long enough and liked it, never care for anything else thereafter.

—Ernest Hemingway

Book One

THE MOUNTAINS 1968

Chapter 1

The peaks of the Allegheny Mountains were invisible, lost in the murky dawn and soiled cloud cover. Large, moist snow flakes fell steadily and without sound, covering the rotting, exhaust-stained mounds of snow alongside the highway. It was the first snow of the new year.

A big tandem diesel was the only vehicle on the six-lane highway for a quarter of a mile in either direction. Its engine rumbled in the stillness. The beating windshield wipers built ridges of snow at the ends of their arcs. The sleepy driver yawned, lifted himself slightly from the seat, and tugged through his pants at his shorts, which had ridden up and were binding his crotch. He settled back down, yawned again, then flipped the direction-signal lever on the side of his steering column.

He double-clutched and began shifting down through the series of gears. The engine noise rose as the truck slowed. Approaching the turnoff, the driver touched the brakes. The compressed air was released in muted plosives and the truck swung gently from the divided highway onto the exit ramp. The driver downshifted again. The truck glided around the curves, passed beneath the highway, and left the ramp to emerge onto an old two-lane road. A green and white sign on the shoulder said *Clairton,* and beneath that, *Population 36,500.*

The town lay in a narrow river valley, built up onto the hillsides. The houses were small, dark little humps in the dim morning and swirling snow.

But neither the snow nor the weak light could conceal, or even diminish, the sprawling bulk and soaring towers of the colossal steel mill that dominated the valley and dwarfed the town, seeming to challenge even the mountains themselves. It spread and turned, angled, arched, and spurred out in a pattern that was too large and complicated for the eye to embrace all at once. It squatted beneath five enormous blast-furnace stacks that towered a full twelve stories into the air, issuing white plumes of smoke. Even lower were the chimneys and hooded vents. Clouds of steam burst from these to billow up and slowly dissipate in the chilly air. Through many of the grimy windows of the plant itself, flashes of fire could be seen.

The driver was shifting up, accelerating, and the RPMs of the engine mounted, growing louder in the cab; still the noise of the great mill began to filter in, muted, but audible even at this distance. Clangs. Hisses. Rumbles. Shrieks. Long, deep groanings.

The driver shook his head, as if to comment on what he saw—as if to express fear of such stupendous industry, to offer thanks to his truck and to the long, open roads on which he spent his days.

He came to a fork. To the right, the road swung off toward the mountains. To the left, it turned in to Division Street, Clairton's main commercial thoroughfare. Almost with reluctance, the driver steered his truck onto Division Street, which was a kind of boundary between the farthest extensions of the steel mill on the west side and the sprawl of ramshackle Victorian houses on the east. The houses were gabled and bay-windowed, and in some cases they seemed prevented from collapse only by the multitude of utility lines that dipped and swayed and crossed and recrossed from house to house, with an occasional stop at a pole when the span was too great. They were dark and drab, and had been built outward and upward onto the foothills on a maze of narrow, zigzagging streets.

Early traffic had turned the snow to slush, and the truck rolled through this with hissing tires and wide, wet sprays. An occasional pedestrian overpass rose across the street to connect the human colony with the great juggernaut on the other side. Across one of these was walking a figure in a lumberjack's plaid mackinaw, watch cap pulled down over his ears and bulky mittens on his hands. The driver caught the man's eyes and lifted his hand from the wheel to wave. The man paused a moment, then offered a curt nod, and went on.

Within the mill, while the truck passed by, destined for a stop at one of the mill's loading docks nearly half a mile away, Michael raised a gloved hand and waggled it.

"Glasses!" he shouted, trying to be heard above the grinding and wrenching.

He slipped his own glasses down from his forehead without glancing back to see if the other four men on his crew had lowered theirs. They were good men. As the turn foreman, he was conscientious in his supervision, but he did not worry about them.

They were on a brick stage in the casting house, several feet above the main level, but far below the spidery network of catwalks and girders that ran beneath the soaring ceiling. They were some distance back from the furnace—a monster of shimmering heat—standing on one of the walkways that were raised up over the deep troughs in the brick stage. They wore asbestos hoods that fell like short tunics down to their waists. Where the hoods stopped, leather aprons began, protecting their lower torsos and legs down to their heavy, steel-toed work boots.

Sweat dripped down Michael's cheeks and throat. His shirt was soaked. He squinted through the dark lenses of his glasses. Frown lines of anticipation appeared on his forehead.

Pure oxygen was jetted into the furnace. A sheet of hellish flame leaped two stories into the air. Michael was buffeted by heat. He set his jaw. Behind him, a massive crane suspended from a gigantic ceiling girder closed its jaws around a white-hot ingot on a stage below, lifted the ingot from its soaking pit, and went screaming away to drop it on a bed of rollers that would carry it on to the next process.

The flame from the top of the furnace abated, flared again, then tapered off and disappeared. Michael picked up a long steel pole and advanced toward the base of the furnace. He braced the pole between his arm and his body and positioned its tip against a black crust that sealed the tap hole at the base of the furnace. He glanced back to see that the members of his crew were standing safely, then hunched his shoulders and drove the pole through the crust.

Molten iron exploded through the opened tap, tearing away the rest of the crust, and gushed into the main trough with a shower of sparks and flame.

Behind Michael, Nick, who was also barely out of his teens, slammed open a heavy sluice gate. The iron went roaring through the trough and branching out into a maze of subchannels.

The crew moved back and forth across the walks above the channels, seeming to elongate and shrink and shimmer in the pulsing waves of heat, checking the flow of metal, opening and closing off channels, freeing blockages with poles.

The flow decreased momentarily, and Michael used the opportunity to tap the walk next to Nick's boot with the end of his pole. Nick looked over. Michael jerked his head toward Steven, the other young member of the crew. He grinned, stripped off a glove, and made a set of cuckold's horns with his hand. Nick offered Steven a similar salute.

Steven smiled, his teeth a stark white line across the grime of his face, and waved them off. Nick raised his hands higher and shook it for emphasis. Steven turned his attention down to a trough, studiously ignoring them.

"Hey!" called Axel, from the other side of Michael. He was a bull of a man, several years older than the others. He pointed. The flow had begun anew, and was lipping over the edges of one of the channels.

Michael signaled Stan, who was Axel's contemporary and the smallest of the crew. Stan opened another channel to relieve the one that was overflowing.

The moment's respite vanished. The men returned to their work with careful concentration.

On the other side of town, partly up a hill, the snow was falling on the green domes of St. Dimitrius's, the Russian Orthodox church. Inside, a young priest with thinning hair was unlocking a cabinet off to the side of an ornately carved altar. Two altar boys were arranging flowers, and an old custodian with liver-spotted hands was polishing the wooden altar rail.

A middleaged woman in a new yellow dress, her hair swept up and stiff with spray, stood at the priest's elbow, fingering the imitation pearls around her neck.

The priest opened the cabinet and removed two

handmade tapers and a pair of golden crowns. He set them on a velvet pillow atop the cabinet.

"Is it all right?" the woman said. "Is everything going to be all right?"

"Yes," the priest answered, with gentle patience.

"Are you sure? You wouldn't lie to me?"

The priest smiled. "No, you know I wouldn't."

"It's just . . . how many times does a first son get married? Once, that's all. Just once. And you want everything to be all right."

The priest nodded.

"It *would* snow," the woman said, twisting the strand of her pearls. "It would. It had to. Everybody's going to slip. Everybody's going to slide. All the cars are going to crash. Oh!"

Her hand went to her mouth and she burst into tears. The priest came to her and put his arms around her.

"I can't believe this," he woman choked. "My own boy . . . with a strange girl I don't even know. And . . . and not so thin, if you understand my meaning. No, not such a thin girl. But it's crazy! Two days later, he's going off to Vietnam!" She sobbed. "He's enlisted. With those crazy friends of his, they enlisted! I don't understand, Father. No, I don't understand nothing anymore. Nothing! Can you explain it? Can anyone explain?"

The priest kissed her forehead and drew back to look at her through wise, sad, comforting eyes. "God will be with them. God watches over His children."

The woman produced a handkerchief from her sleeve. She wiped her eyes and blew her nose.

"Yes," she said. "Yes. I know, Father. Thank you, Father."

The graveyard shift was ending. Steam whistles blew every seven minutes, releasing blocks of workers in staggered sections. Still, bottlenecks built in the huge changing shed, where long lines of men with soot-darkened faces and layers of sweaty clothes queued up before the time clocks ranked on the long wall. Many still wore their hard hats, goggles pushed up over the visors. They were mostly big and physical men, and their humor was loud and rough.

Michael was one of the first to clock out. He was a young man of medium height and modest build, but graceful and sinewy. He was dark-complexioned, with short, jet-black hair. His face was built in planes. It was handsome, in a subdued and quiet fashion. It was a quiet face, friendly, but private, and at moments almost shy.

Steven was right behind him, holding his own card. And Nick punched out simultaneously with him on the next clock over.

They were about Michael's age, a little taller, a touch heavier, and their Slavic heritage a bit more visible in their broad cheekbones and solid jaws. They had graduated from high school together and had gone to work immediately at the steel mill, as almost all the young men in Clairton did. And already it seemed as if they had spent the bulk of their lives there. It was that, and boredom, and the patriotism of anyone raised in the blue-collar Americanism of a small town. A steel town, where parents and grandparents still remembered the oppression and poverty of the countries of their childhoods and were feverishly loyal to their new land. All that had caused them to enlist.

More than a thousand men were clocking out, pulling on parkas and jackets, pressing through the exits into the snowdrifts of the large parking lot, and hundreds more were coming off their shift by the minute.

A wind had kicked up, swirling the snow. Michael clamped the collar of his coat closed around his throat with one hand as he left the shed.

"Where's Stan?" Nick asked.

Michael looked around. "He wasn't far behind us at the clocks. He should be out in a minute."

Steven pointed. "There's Axel. Hey, Axel!"

Axel towered over a cluster of men. He was fully six and a half feet tall, a boisterous, enormously powerful juggernaut of a man with the serene smile of an angel, and a gut half the size of a wheelbarrow. He veered toward them and plowed through the streaming river of men like a river barge.

He wrapped a long arm around Steven's shoulders. "How you feeling, Steven?"

"I feel okay."

Deadpan, Axel asked, "You feelin' hot?"

Steven cuffed him on the shoulder and grinned. But there was uncertainty in his face. Not about Axel, whom he liked, but over something else, something vague, something he couldn't define, something that was not settled: he had left his boyhood behind, but had yet to settle comfortably into manhood.

Nick winked. "Watch out, Axel. We'll be calling him 'Old Fire Balls' after tonight."

"Fuckin' A," Axel said.

"There's Stan."

"Stan!" Nick shouted. "Over here!"

"Stan!" Steve yelled.

Carried along in the general press moving toward the cars, Stan swiveled his head, but couldn't locate them.

"Go get him, Axel," Michael said.

"Right."

Axel waded into the steelworkers and bulled his way back out with Stan. The five men hunched up against the wind and snow and started off through the parking lot.

"Jesus," Steven said. He stopped and craned his head back. "Look at that. I never saw anything like that before. What the hell is it?"

The others looked up. A perfect halo circled the dim white sun, hazy through the snow and cloud cover, and at four points on the outer rim of the halo—top, bottom, and sides—were four shimmering little discs, each a miniature replica of the sun itself.

"Sun dogs," Michael said. "Holy shit. Sun dogs!"

The men stood looking up in wondering silence.

Axel said, "What're sun dogs?"

"A sign," Michael said. "A blessing on the hunters sent by the Great Wolf to his children."

Stan screwed up his face. "What the fuck are you talking about?"

"It's an old Indian thing."

"You're full of shit."

"Would I shit you about a thing like that?" Michael asked with a smile.

Stan studied Michael's face, trying to determine whether or not Michael was putting him on. He shook his head. "Mike, there's sometimes nobody but a doctor can understand you."

"It's an omen," Mike said. He rubbed his jaw. "Jesus, could we have ourselves one great fuckin' hunting trip tonight."

Nick said, "Goddamn, Mike, I don't know where you pick up all this shit."

Michael shrugged. "It'll be a good night. I guarantee it."

Steven looked at him incredulously. "Wait a minute, Mike. Don't tell me. Don't tell me you're honestly thinking about going deer hunting?"

Michael shrugged again. The others looked somewhat embarrassed. They resumed walking through the parking lot. Michael's ten-year-old dented and rusty Cadillac Coup de Ville was sixty yards ahead of them, a drift of snow halfway up the driver's side.

"Not tonight!" Steven said emphatically. "Oh no, you guys. I'm getting married tonight, for Christ's sake. You fuckin' guys would go up deer hunting while I'm getting married? I don't goddamn believe it."

Stan said, "Hey, we'd get you legal. We'd get you all tucked in bed with Angela first. I mean, what the hell would be wrong with that?" He looked to the others. "Right? Am I right?"

"Fuckin' A," Alex said.

"You guys are crazy," Steven said, with sudden envy. "You know that? I mean, you guys are fuckin' nuts!"

"You're getting married, and *we're* nuts. I like that."

Nick put an arm around Steven. "It's all right. Hey, it's all right, don't get your back up. We'll be right there with you. All of us." He turned to the others. "Won't we? Right? Am I right?"

"Right," said Michael.

"Fuckin' A!" said Axel.

Chapter 2

They pushed and shoved and danced around each other all the way to Michael's car, jollying Steven out of his pique. He was laughing with them as they kicked the snowdrift away from the doors.

"Come on," Nick said. "Come on, you guys, get in. I'm buying the first round this morning."

He and Nick threw Steven into the back seat, then piled in after him. Axel got into the front seat beside Michael. The engine sputtered and coughed a few times, then turned over—to cheers from the rear seat —and idled roughly, in need of tuning. Michael revved it. Blue oil smoke misted up behind them in a cloud. Michael put the car in gear and nosed into the line of other vehicles headed for the main gate.

"Hey, Steven," Stan said. "Any help you might need tonight, I want you to feel free to call on me."

"Sometimes your sense of humor ain't funny, Stanley."

"C'mon, Steven," Nick said.

"Willing fingers," Stan said.

Michael glanced back over his shoulder: "Extra lips . . ."

"Fuckin' A!" said Axel, pounding a fist into his thigh.

"You know, Axel," Nick said, "you're a regular poet, you're so eloquent."

"I couldn't agree with you more," Axel said.

Michael squinted through the streaked arcs the wipers cut in the dirt and snow on the windshield. He saw an opening in the parked cars, cut the wheel hard left, and shot down another lane. The car bounced and rocked as it hit potholes, spraying slush into the air. Michael ran the lane, then cut sharply back into the line in front of a Pinto, having jumped a good dozen cars nearer the exit.

"All right!" Stan said.

Several minutes passed before they inched up to the exit. There was a *Caution* sign at the gate, but no one ever paid any attention to it, and Michael went spinning out into the narrow end of Division Street, hanging a left.

The blast of an airhorn startled them. A big tractor-trailer was emerging from the underpass just behind them, where the railroad that ran parallel to Division curved up over the street. The truck swung to the left of the Cadillac to avoid them.

"Stand on it!" Axel yelled.

A rock wall was to their right, the truck to their

left, out in the lane for oncoming traffic. The thing for Michael to do was brake and allow the truck to slip back in ahead of them. There wasn't room for anything else.

"Stand on it!" Axel repeated.

"*You'd* never do it," Stan said with excitement.

Michael stamped the accelerator down.

Axel swiveled around to glare at Stan. "Are you accusin' me of somethin?"

Michael gripped the wheel tightly. "Shut the hell up! I'm trying to concentrate!"

"Go, babe!" Nick said.

"Stand on it, stand on it!"

"Hit it, man!"

The Cadillac's right wheels slammed over the curb, bouncing them all up and jolting them back down into the sprung seats. The car barrelled along at an angle, two wheels on the street and two on the sidewalk, the right side inches away from scraping along the rock wall. On their left was the bulk of the tractor-trailer, its airhorn blaring frantically. A telephone pole next to the wall was coming up rapidly.

Nick had his glove off and was staring at the second hand of his watch.

"How we doing?" Michael said tensely.

"Never happen!" Nick said. "You can't make it!"

"Yeah?" Mike hunched forward and said, "Go! Go!" to the car.

Nick threw a piece of paper over Michael's shoulder.

"What's that?" Michael said.

"Registration. My pickup against your Caddy."

"Uh-oh, uh-oh," Alex was saying, staring at the telephone pole.

Michael didn't move his eyes. "Today your lucky day?"

"It's always my lucky day."

"We're gonna hit it," Axel said, bracing his hands against the dashboard.

Michael half-lifted from his seat as he stood on the accelerator. He jammed a hand against the horn and swung left, scraping against the side of the tractor-trailer, missing the telephone pole by a hair. Then he cut right again onto the sidewalk, pulled ahead of the truck's cab, and swung back onto the street once more.

"Oh, Jesus!" Steven said with relief.

Michael spun the wheel left again and hit the brakes. The Cadillac slewed across the opposite lane through a break in the oncoming traffic and spun end around end, then came to a halt spraying slush up against the lettered window of John Welch's bar.

The truck roared on by, airhorn blasting, the driver shaking a fist at them, his face contorted with rage.

Steve, Nick, and Stan cheered from the back seat.

"Fuckin' A!" Axel said. He gave the finger to the disappearing truck.

Michael handed Nick his registration back. "I'd be taking advantage of you. You should have had odds. You were offering even money against a sure thing." He gave Nick a spare smile.

"There's no such thing as a sure thing," Nick said.

The VFW Hall was an old whitewashed building with high, arched windows. The walls of the main room which was long and rectangular, with a small stage at one end, were painted in pastoral scenes: cows grazing in a field, a steepled church in winter, mountainscapes. There was a trophy case near the entrance with battle ribbons, letters of commendation, and photographs of young men in antiquated uniforms with their arms around each others' shoulders, sitting or standing near artillery, tanks, the rubble of buildings. Behind the arch of the stage, a big American flag hung down from the ceiling.

On the wall above the arch were big blown-up photographs of Michael, Steven, and Nick. Their hair was very short, their faces thinner and younger. They were the graduation photos from their high school year book. A block-lettered sign tacked above the photos said: *Serving God and Country Proudly.*

Two white-haired men stood on stepladders holding red-white-and-blue bunting which they were about to tape to the borders of the photos.

Two other elderly men, shrunken and knobby-jointed, wearing heavy glasses, one with a single lens blacked out, looked up at them.

"Up, I would say," the man with the black lens commented. "What would you say?"

His companion agreed. "Up."

The men on the ladders lifted the bunting higher.

A handful of gray-haired women were spreading white paper tablecloths over the trestle tables and setting up folding chairs.

"Closer in to Steven's picture," said the old veteran with the blacked lens.

His friend said, "Down a bit, I would say. What would you say?"

"Down."

"Down a bit," said the first man.

The men on the ladders lowered the bunting.

The outer door opened and a blast of cold air with a swirl of snow blew in. Half a dozen women in their fifties and sixties entered, bulkily dressed in heavy, dark coats, galoshes, and scarves. Two of them carried a high, tiered wedding cake topped with figurines of a bride and groom. The other women hovered about them, steadying them.

"Careful, now."

"Watch your step."

"Don't let it tilt!"

They carried the cake to a table in the center of the room and set it down, then stood back to admire it. The old veterans and the other women came over to them.

"It's beautiful."

"Oh! It makes me want to cry."

"They're very lucky to have such a nice cake."

The new arrivals stamped snow from their boots, chafed their hands together, and rubbed their cheeks. Suddenly, the oldest of them tottered and fell.

Someone brought a chair. They sat her in it, opened her coat, removed her gloves and boots, and rubbed her hands and ankles.

"Here. This will help." The one-eyed man brought a tumblerfull of wine.

The woman took it, held it under her nose a moment

sniffing, and rocked back and forth in the chair, saying, "Ah, ah. It's so cold."

She lifted the wine to her lips, tilted her head, and drained it with a series of loud wallows, not lowering the glass until it was empty.

"Dot's better," she said with a wide grin. "Dot's much better!"

Angela had come to Steven's house early in the morning with her suitcases and a small cardboard box filled with the souvenirs and mementos of her childhood. Steven's father had died several years ago. Steven was the youngest child in the family and the only one still living at home. Since Angela was the oldest of five children and her own house was cramped and overfull anyway, it was decided that she would move into Steven's house and live with his mother until he returned from military service.

The room was poorly lit, the wallpaper old and faded, and Angela didn't like it at all and hoped she would have another room to live in.

But it wasn't the room; she was perceptive enough to realize that. It was the strangeness of the house—smells that she hadn't grown up with, turns in the halls she wasn't used to, cushions on the furniture whose contours were unfamiliar to her body. It was all different. It wasn't what she knew. And she was pregnant. She was frightened and upset and confused.

She was already in her wedding dress. She picked up her veil, put it on her head, and went over to look in the mirror suspended from two posts that rose from the dresser top.

Was she pretty?

She tried to look at herself through Steven's eyes, through the eyes of Steven's mother, through the eyes of their friends.

She didn't know.

She sucked in her breath to flatten her belly, which was already prominently rounded. It didn't work.

"Oh, God!" she said.

She ignored her belly, looked into her own eyes.

"I do," she said, with deep sincerity.

She shook her head, squeezed her eyes shut a moment, then opened them again.

"I do," she said with heartfelt passion.

She scowled.

"I do," she said shyly, coyly.

She breathed deeply.

"I do— Oh! I do, I do, I do. Oh!"

She whirled and flung herself down on the bed. She sniffled, bunched up the spread, and buried her face in it, fighting tears. She felt a little better after she had cried for a couple of minutes.

She sat up and probed in her open suitcase for a packet of tissues. She came up with a square of cardboard, about the size of the ones you sometimes found in new shirts. On it was written, *This is it—more or less. Love, Mom.*

She turned it over. On it was taped a photograph that had been cut from a magazine. It was a photograph of Michelangelo's *David,* proud, muscled, beautiful, naked.

"Oh, my God," she said.

* * *

John Welch's bar was packed with boisterous steelworkers. The jukebox blared. A sports broadcaster on the television set over the door announced that the Philadelphia Eagles were beating the Oakland Raiders 14 to 0. Cigar and cigarette smoke hung in thick layers around the many deer heads mounted on the walls, the lacquered trout and bass fixed to walnut and mahogany boards, the stuffed pheasant and quail, and the red fox mounted with his paws on a piece of tree limb, sightless glass eyes fixed on empty space. There were framed photographs of men in red plaid jackets, holding guns, next to deer suspended from trees and lashed over car fenders; the carcass of a black bear was tied to the luggage rack atop a station wagon.

Michael and his crew trooped in.

John Welch hollered, "Well, look who's here!" and came out from behind the bar. He wrapped Steven in a bear hug and began bouncing him up and down. Welch was a couple of years older than Steven—in his late twenties—and nearly as big as Axel. He hooted.

Men left their barstools and tables to gather around. They banged Steven on the shoulder, thumped him on the back, and swatted his head, congratulating him.

Steven endured all this with embarrassed good humor. Welch released him. Men began thrusting glasses at him.

"On me, Steve. This is your last day as a free man."

"Have a drink, Steve, you're gonna need your strength tonight."

Nick glanced up at the television set. "Hey!" he shouted. "I got a hundred bucks that says the Eagles never cross the fifty in the next half—and Oakland wins by 20."

Axel had picked a half-empty pitcher of beer from the bar, and downed what was left of it in a series of big gulps. He put the pitcher back and wiped foam from his mouth with the back of his hand.

Stan yelled, "And I got another twenty that says the Eagles' quarterback wears a dress."

"Fuckin' A!" Axel said, and then he began to cry.

Chapter 3

Linda was in her bridesmaid's dress in the kitchen. She was a slim, nearly fragile girl, with a pale, oval face framed by long, raven hair. She was hauntingly pretty, but now her forehead was creased with lines of worry and she bit down on her lower lip. She was looking up at the ceiling.

Thumping noises sounded from the bedroom above. They grew louder. There was a crash, then another, as furniture was hurled about. Then a loud thud, followed by silence.

Linda shook her head. She went to the cabinet, took out a tray, and laid it on the counter next to the stove. She put a plate and a cup and saucer on it, laid silverware and a napkin beside the plate. She put two slices of bread into the toaster, then ladled stew from a pot on the stove onto the plate. She dropped a tea bag into the cup and poured hot water over it. When the toast popped up, she buttered it and set the slices along the edge of the plate. She lifted the tray and carried it out of the kitchen, up the stairs, and to the closed door. She knocked.

There was no answer.

She pushed the door open and entered.

The room was a wreck. Chairs were turned over, a lamp was smashed, pictures hung at odd angles on the wall. One had fallen and suffered a broken frame. A window was open, and wind and snow blew in.

Her father was lying face-down in the middle of the room, still in his coat, which was torn and muddy. He had lost a shoe somewhere. He held a partly empty bottle in his hand, which was dribbling its contents onto the rug.

Linda set the tray on the bed and went down on one knee beside her father. "Daddy?"

He mumbled and rolled over and looked at her, blinking.

She touched his shoulder. "Daddy?"

He pushed himself up to a sitting position. He looked out the open window, across the crooked roofs of other houses to the looming bulk of the mill, and the acres of steelworkers' cars in the vast, snowy parking lot.

"Go to fucking hell," he muttered. "I'll give every car in the town a flat tire. Every goddamn car. I'll do it."

Linda worked her hands into his armpits and strained to lift him. He rose unsteadily, wobbled with her to the bed, and sat on the edge. He turned his head slowly to look into her face. His skin was gray and doughy. He hadn't shaved. A long, crusty cut with the black knots of stitches still in it ran across the left side of his forehead. A line of saliva dipped from the corner of his mouth.

"I mean what I say, girl. All around, like a sea! Like an ocean of flat tires."

"Yes, Daddy."

She left him to close the window. As she drew the sash down, he rolled off the bed and fell to the floor.

Linda hiked up her dress, bent and pulled one of his arms around her shoulders, strained to get him back up on the bed. She wrestled with him for several moments before she managed it. It was a large effort; she was breathing heavily and there were tears in her eyes.

He fell down again.

"Oh, Daddy!" she cried.

She tried once more, using the last of her strength, and pushing herself beyond even that.

Her father struck out suddenly, catching her full in the face, and sending her reeling backward. She fell over a chair to the floor.

"Fucking bitch . . . all bitches!" Her father pushed himself up and lurched toward her.

Linda stood and held out her hands to him. "Daddy! Daddy, it's me, Linda!"

He rocked her head with a slap. Her vision jumped and her ears rang. She raised her hands to block his next blow, but he got through and slapped her again.

"I hate 'em! Fucking bitches! I'll give 'em all flat tires . . ."

He missed with a roundhouse blow, spun around, and collapsed on the floor again, mumbling incoherently.

Tears ran down Linda's cheeks. She stood crying quietly.

"Fuckin' bitches. All of you!" her father slurred into the rug.

Linda walked out and went down the hall into her room, and took a suitcase from her closet.

Michael, Nick, Steven, and Axel were leaning forward over the bar, while big John Welch inclined his head toward theirs from the other side. They were all trying to harmonize with the Dolly Parton song on the jukebox. Only John, whose voice was lovely, succeeded, but they had drunk too much to know the difference, and were having a whale of a good time.

Stan was arguing with a fat teamster over whose turn it was to use the pool table. The argument was growing heated.

The bar was still full of noisy, drinking men.

A screech sounded from the back room.

John stopped singing and walked to the end of the bar. No one else seemed to notice.

A waitress burst through the swinging doors. "There's a crazy woman in there!" she cried.

"What?" John said.

The teamster grabbed Stan by the shoulders and threw him against the wall. "How 'bout I bounce you up and down like a basketball, Shorty?"

Something broke in the back room and a couple of men turned their heads toward the doors.

Stan's hand darted under his shirt to his waistband and whipped back out holding a snubnosed revolver that he pointed at the teamster's belly. "How 'bout you get the fuck outta here, fat man?"

The teamster's eyes widened and he began to back off.

The doors to the back room banged open just as John was reaching for them. The nearest one caught him in the forehead.

"Yow!" He jerked back, holding his head.

Steven's mother charged out, swinging a board. "What is this?" she yelled. "Drinking all morning on your wedding day! Get out, get out!"

She flailed about with the board. Men ducked out of her way. She knocked drinks from the bar, turned over chairs. She raged like a fury, swatting the board against the backs and legs of dodging men.

There was a general rush for the door, loud howls of protest, and much hilarity.

Steven, Nick, Michael, and Axel ran out together, stood in falling snow.

"Boy, this is it," Steven said. "This is really it. I mean—here I go!"

Nick laughed. "Just as well she got you out. There's no sense in your getting *too* relaxed, Steven."

"Fuckin' A," Axel said drunkenly.

Steven's mother emerged, flushed, still grimly gripping her board. She looked at Steven, let the board slip from her hands, and started to cry.

"My beautiful boy. My angel . . . who is leaving his own mother for a strange girl . . . a pregnant girl!" She rushed to Steven and threw herself into his arms.

"Momma . . ."

"So cold is your heart to do this to your own mother, a person who goes to mass twice a day all her life?"

"Momma, we'll be all right. We'll be right upstairs. We'll have a family again."

He looked with intense embarrassment at his friends, who gave him expressions of sympathy, then busied themselves studying snowflakes.

"So cruel is your heart? Is your heart so uncaring? You marry this girl, leave me with her. Then you run off to Vietnam?"

"It's one flight, Momma," Steven said wearily, having gone through this several times before. "One flight. I'll be living right upstairs when I come home." He paused. "I love Angela, Ma. She loves me."

His mother didn't say anything.

"It's true," he said.

After a moment of silence, she said, "Wear a scarf today."

He made a face. "I'm not wearing a scarf with a tuxedo. You don't wear a scarf with a tuxedo!"

It was getting on toward noon. Michael pressed the accelerator down as he approached the driveway that led up the hill to the trailer he shared with Nick. The car picked up speed, 20, 25, 30, 35, then he was starting up, continuing an even pressure on the accelerator, the back tires spitting out snow and slush, the Caddy beginning to fishtail. He swung the wheel in short little arcs, compensating for the rear-end swing. As he neared the crest, the wheels began to spin, and he slammed the car down into a lower gear and gunned the motor. Slipping and sliding, the engine roaring, the Caddy made it the final distance to level ground. He braked, turned the motor off, and pulled out the hand brake.

He got out of the car in his rented tuxedo, feeling as weird as a trained animal in costume. Incongruously, he was wearing his mountain boots, the cuffs of his pants tucked into their tops. He carried his dress shoes in his hand. He slogged through the wet snow around Nick's battered old pickup truck. There were empty rifle racks across the rear window of the pickup's cab.

The trailer was a two-tone silver job, stained along the seams with silicone caulk and marred with roofing tar that had slopped down from the top. They'd bought it third-hand from a construction site. It stood on cinder blocks on a knoll overlooking the town and the mill. It wasn't much to look at, but they'd managed to make it weathertight, and it was home, and they liked it well enough.

Michael kicked snow out of the way and pulled the door open.

Nick was in his dress pants and starched shirt, sitting on the couch, his tuxedo jacket hanging over the back of a chair beside him. He was rubbing mink oil onto his field boots by hand.

"You trying to look like a prince?" he asked Michael.

"What do you mean trying?"

He laughed.

"You should've waterproofed those last night," Michael said.

"I know."

"That way it sets."

"Yeah, I know that, Mike."

Michael went to the refrigerator, got out a can of beer, and opened it. He leaned against the counter that served as a divider between the kitchen and the living room, sipping. He looked around the trailer, feeling the first twinges of nostalgia. In two days he would be gone, and it would be a long time before he would be back.

A deerhead was mounted over the sink, an eleven-pointer. Burlap curtains. Racked rifles on the living room wall. Furniture they'd scrounged from relatives and friends. Fishing rods in the corner. The new vinyl they'd laid on the kitchen floor. Back packs and sleeping bags piled in the corner. Hunting prints in dime-store frames. The skinning knife he'd sharpened yesterday was still out on the kitchen table, next to the hard Arkansas stone. The box of Norma Power-Point .30-60 cartridges atop the refrigerator. He liked it all.

"I just wait," he said. "You know?"

"Huh?"

"I just wait," he repeated. "For this . . . it's what I wait for. The mountains. It's the only place I've ever really felt right, felt good. I wait all year to get to the mountains, to the deer."

Nick picked up an old toothbrush, rubbed it across the lardlike mink oil, then began working the dressing into the seam between the sides and sole of a boot.

"So do I," he said. "I guess."

"You do?" Michael said.

"Yeah. What the hell . . . I think about it. I think about Vietnam, too."

Abruptly, he set aside his boots, wiped his hands on a paper towel, got up and took a scoped, bolt-action rifle down from the rack. He opened a drawer at the bottom of the rack and removed a clean chamois cloth. He began stripping excess oil off the gun.

"You really think about it?" Michael asked.

"Yeah. I don't know." He shook his head. "For Christ's sake, Mike, Steven's getting married in a couple of hours. I don't know what the hell we're even doing talking about hunting a last time before the army. The whole thing's crazy." He slid the bolt out of the gun and peered down the barrel. He replaced the bolt and sat down with the rifle across his knees. He looked out the window. "Fuck," he said.

Michael swigged from his beer. "I'll tell you one thing. If I found out my life had to end up in the mountains, it would be all right, you know?" Nick turned to face him. "But it has to be there, in your mind," Michael said.

"What? One shot?"

Michael smiled. "Two is pussy."

Nick looked back out the window. "I don't think about one shot that much anymore, Mike."

"You have to," Michael said with passion. "A deer should be taken with one shot. One shot is what it's all about. You try to tell people. But they won't listen." He was silent a moment. "You really think about Vietnam?"

"I don't know. I guess I'm thinking about the deer . . . or maye going to 'Nam. I don't know. I think about it all." Nick set the rifle aside, braced his elbows on his knees, clasped his hands, and leaned forward. "I like the way the trees are in the mountains," he said. "All the different ways the trees are. I sound like some asshole, right?"

"I'll tell you something, Nick. I wouldn't hunt with anyone but you. I like guys with quick moves and speed. I won't hunt with an asshole."

Nick laughed. "Who's an asshole?"

"Who's an asshole? Who do you think's an asshole?" He gestured toward the window, and the town and the mill beyond. "They're all assholes. I mean, they're all great guys, for Christ's sake, but . . . the point is, Nick, without you, I'd hunt alone. Seriously. I would. That's what I'd do."

Nick grinned and made a motion with his hand as if to push everything away. "You're a fuckin' nut. You know that, Mike? You're a maniac control-freak."

Michael grinned back. "I just don't like surprises."

A horn sounded from outside. Michael went to the door. "It's Axel and John."

Nick stepped outside with Michael.

Axel and John were both in tuxes that were much too small and tight for them. They looked like Tweedledum and Tweedledee blown up to giant proportions. They had backpacks, rifles, and parkas with them, and they were pounding on the trunk of Michael's Caddy.

"Axel!" Nick said. "John! For Christ's sake—wait a minute, you guys."

Axel, drunk, roared, "It won't open!"

Michael trooped through the snow and pointed. "You gotta kick it here. *Here,* Axel, not there."

"Where should I kick it? Just show me where I should kick it."

"Here," Michael said. "Kick it here."

Axel narrowed his eyes, stepped back, raised his leg, and drove his shoe like a hydraulic ram against the trunk.

The lid popped open.

"Fuckin' A!" Axel said.

"All right!" John said. "Too bad you're not still kicking like that for the Steelers." He jerked his head up. "Oops! I mean, I didn't mean, uh—"

"Right. Sure. Uh-huh," Axel said, trying to brush the remark aside. "You know, I love Mike's car. Some cars sit, you know. But this car, a car like this . . . grows. I mean, you never know with a car like this. You never know *where* this car is going."

"Yeah," Nick said. "It makes me feel safe."

Michael gave Nick a long, sober look.

Axel went to his car, out of which Stan was climbing with his pack slung over one shoulder and his rifle in hand. Axel got a beer from the sixpack on the front seat, popped the top, and raised the can.

"Salud," he said, then started to chugalug the beer.

"Hey, someone give me a hand," Stan said.

Unlike the others, his tux looked as if it had been hand-tailored for him. His shoes gleamed and he was trying to pussyfoot through the snow toward the Caddy.

"Shhh!" John said. "Axel's gonna hump Mike's Coupe de Ville."

Axel took the can from his mouth and looked at John, then turned to the Caddy.

There was a little beer left in the can. He upended

the can and poured what remained of the beer over the trunk.

"In Nomine Patri, et Filii, et Spiritu Sancti," he said, dredging up his old altar boy Latin. "Amen."

He tossed the empty can over his shoulder, puffed out his chest, and pounded on it with his fists. He let loose a magnificent, yodeling Tarzan yell.

A four-door Chevy was struggling up the drive to the trailer. There were five girls in it, wearing pale green bridesmaids' dresses. The car topped the hill and came to a halt as Axel finished his yell.

Echoes came bouncing back from the mountains, and Axel looked pleased. As the echoes faded, the church bell began to ring down the hill.

"Eeeee—aaahhh!" Axel screamed.

He threw himself against the Caddy, clawed at the roof with his hands, and banged his hips back and forth against the door.

"Axel!" said the first girl out of the Chevy. *"What are you doing?"*

The other girls got out, stepping gingerly in the snow and making faces at Axel.

Axel smiled broadly. "I have a deep and intense relationship with this car."

A blonde girl said, "Come on, you guys, hurry up! We're going to be late."

"Who's got the carnations?" one of the girls asked.

"I do," answered the girl next to her. "They're here, right here." She opened a shoebox.

The first girl looked at Axel with a frown. "You're a mess," she said.

"But a lovable mess," he answered.

"Someone put his carnation on."

"Who's got hands? My hands are frozen."

The girls straightened ties and adjusted cummerbunds.

One of them pinned Axel's carnation on his lapel. "Boy," she said, "this crummy tuxedo's been stuck with a million flowers. Where'd you get this thing? Look at all the holes in the lapel!"

"Fuckin' A!" Axel said proudly.

"Nick," someone said softly, almost whispering.

Nick swiveled his head.

Linda was standing at the corner of the trailer, apart from the others and out of their line of sight. She had a suitcase in her hand.

Nick went to her. "Hi. Watcha doin' back here?"

"Hi." She smiled weakly at him. "Your shoes are soaking." Then her smile vanished and she pressed her lips together.

"Hey, what's the matter?"

She shook her head, swirling her hair, and wouldn't look at him.

"You want to talk?"

"Can . . . can we go inside?"

"Sure."

Nick led her into the trailer and cleared a space for her on the couch.

"What's going on?"

Linda started to speak, stopped, then breathed deeply, and squared her shoulders. "I was just wondering," she said slowly, picking her words carefully. "You and Michael, you're both going into the army in a couple of days with Steven. If I could use this place to stay until you guys come back, because . . . well, if I could, that's all."

"Sure. Are you kidding? For sure."

"I'd want to pay you both."

Nick knelt on one knee in front of her and took her hands. "Linda. Hey, Linda."

"No," she said, shaking her head. "I would want to pay you."

"Linda, Linda."

She lifted her eyes to his. "What?" she asked in a small voice.

Nick held her hands, unable to say what he wanted to. "I don't know . . ."

Chapter 4

Steven and Angela stood facing each other before the small altar. Behind them, Linda held one of the golden crowns above Angela's head, and Nick held the other above Steven's head.

In the choir loft, a chorus of men was singing the Russian wedding hymn: deep, haunting music that summoned up images of the endless steppes, of dim cathedrals, of icons, incense, and longing. Big John Welch's quavering baritone seemed to carry the entire choir.

"Blessed be the Kingdom," the priest intoned, "now and forever, unto ages and ages."

In the second row of the congregation, opposite the bridesmaids, were Michael, Stan, and Axel, kneeling awkwardly in their tight tuxedoes, wriggling their toes with the cold, wet leather of their snow-soaked shoes. Behind them were ranked the pews of the other celebrants, men and women dressed in their best, which had been carefully cleaned and pressed for the occasion. Their faces and hands were lined and work-worn. There was the hardness of survivors in their expressions, but the day and the ceremony had suffused them with a kind of tenderness, a community of heart.

The priest handed a taper to Angela and another to Steven.

Across from each other, Nick and Linda looked in one another's eyes, gazing in timid amazement.

The priest lit Angela's taper, turned and touched the match to Steven's. Flanked by the burning tapers, he lifted his hands and said to the assembly, "For everyone that does evil hates the light, and does not come to the light, lest his deeds will be reproved. . . ."

He finished, then motioned to Michael's pew, and to the bridesmaids. They came up to the altar; the girls gathered around Angela, the young men around Steven. The girls touched their hands to the crown as the priest lowered it onto Angela's head, and Michael and the other ushers assisted in the crowning of Steven.

The priest said, "The servant of God, Steven, is crowned for the servant of God, Angela, in the Name of the Father and of the Son and of the Holy Ghost. Amen."

He joined Steven's and Linda's hands and led them around the altar in a circle to signify that their union would hold for eternity. The bridesmaids and the ushers followed after them.

As they completed the circle, Michael and Linda came face-to-face with each other. He looked deep into her eyes. She returned his gaze for a moment, then faltered and looked away.

The thumping band music was nearly deafening in the crowded VFW Hall. The tables and chairs had been pushed back to the walls and couples were whirling about, vying for space, colliding with one another, switching partners, and spinning away. There were lines at the two tables from which drinks and food were being served by middle-aged and elderly women, who filled glasses and plates with great speed, but seemingly never fast enough. Knots of older men stood smoking in corners, conferring with great seriousness or laughing raucously and salaciously.

Michael stood alone with a can of beer on the side of the dancers, watching his friends flow past him: Angela laughing up at Steven, Linda clinging softly to Nick, Stan with a thirtyish, buxomy woman with dyed, flaming red hair, John Welch nuzzling a chubby girl who giggled, and Axel wrapping up the blonde bridesmaid (Beth was her name, Michael thought) in a raunchy bearhug. Michael drank his beer with stiff, quick gulps.

As the band ended its tune, several of the older women began clinking forks against their glasses. The sound spread quickly, and in moments the entire hall was alive with it, and nothing else could be heard.

Steven looked around, grinned, gathered Angela in his arms, lifting her feet from the floor, and kissed her passionately.

The hall broke into whistles, foot-stamping, and applause.

The band began another tune.

Michael got rid of his empty and pulled a new can from the ice-packed barrel behind him. He saw a plain, quiet-looking girl with lustrous brown hair sitting on a chair against the wall to the side of the barrel. She smiled at him. He averted his eyes, pretending not to see, and edged to the other side of a post, staring up at his high school photo, which rested between Steven's and Nick's likenesses, on the wall. He studied the face intently, trying to remember exactly who that boy had been.

The dance ended. The old women in the hall began to sing, as two of them carried the wedding cake from the kitchen out to a table. People began to gather around. Steven's mother faced Angela across the table, both looking at the "bride and groom" figures atop the cake. They looked up at the same moment. Strained smiles appeared on their mouths. They held this expression for several moments, then Angela suddenly reached out and took the figures from the cake. She stretched out her arm and gave them to Steven's mother. The older woman looked at them dumbly a moment, then burst into tears. They both hurried to the end of the table. They fell into each other's arms, weeping and sobbing and kissing each other.

The cake was cut. The liquor continued to flow. When everyone had eaten a piece of the cake, the band began anew. The loud, thumping polka music and stamping feet made the floor and walls vibrate.

John Welch stood at the end of the coat racks, in front of the dancing area, with a wicker basket filled with money and envelopes. Beside him, swaying drunkenly, was Axel, holding a tray on which there were shotglasses full of whiskey, and some cigars wrapped in cellophane.

As a new couple passed in front of them, John extended the basket.

"What's this?" said the man.

"For a buck," Axel said, beaming, "you get a shot, a cigar, and a dance with the beautiful bride."

The man dug in his pocket and dropped a dollar into John's basket. Axel handed him a shot, took back the empty after the man had drained it, and stuck a cigar in the man's breast pocket. He called to Angela, who came twirling over with her dance partner.

"Give him a dance, beautiful," he said.

Angela put her arms around the man, spun off with him for a few seconds, then left him for another man who beckoned, and went dancing away with her hand held out a little so the people she passed could admire her ring.

At the end of the number, the bandleader stepped forward to the microphone. "Quiet! Quiet, please!" he said. "Could I have your attention, please."

Slowly the hubbub subsided.

The bandleader said, "Angela and Steven would like to welcome you and introduce you to their bridal party, and especially to Nick and Michael who are also going to Vietnam with Steven to proudly serve their country."

A tremendous burst of applause swept over the room. Someone turned on a spotlight that illuminated the area in front of the stage. Steven and Angela appeared in it, motioning for their party to join them.

The bridesmaids and ushers came forward. The band struck up "The Stars and Stripes Forever." Everyone stood in solemn quiet.

When it was over, the old women banged their forks against their glasses. The sound rose to a crescendo. Steven kissed Angela again accompanied by a round of cheers.

The band began a two-step. Steven and Angela started the dance, the bridal party came after them. Michael found himself with Linda. He held her stiffly.

Nick, with Beth, the blonde girl, gave Michael a little shove as he went by. "Relax, old buddy, she doesn't bite."

Michael moved across the floor with Linda. They looked at each other. Her nostrils were flared and her breath was quicker than one would have thought. Michael danced with great formality.

"I'm not the best at this," he said.

"You're doing fine."

He nodded. Some little distance separated their bodies, and he made sure they came no closer.

After what he felt was a respectable time, he said, "Whew, It's getting to me, finally. I bet you could use a break, too. Would you like a beer?"

"Sure," she said, to agree with him.

"What kind of beer would you like?"

She laughed. "I don't know, Michael. I don't really care. Beer is beer."

"I'll get you a Miller's," he said earnestly. "Miller's High Life. That's the best there is." He hurried away from her.

The barrel was nearly empty. Michael had to grope

in the freezing water and what remained of the ice to find two cans. Men came from the kitchen with new cases as he attempted to dry his hands on the wet towel that hung over the side of the barrel.

Nick appeared before the plain girl on the chair to the side of the barrel. She did not seem to have moved all evening. Nick said something to her. She blushed, then smiled and nodded, and stood up and walked to the dance floor with him. They went whirling off. She threw her head back and laughed, and her face became luminous and animated.

Michael watched them for a moment, then went back to Linda. She was sitting down. He pulled up a chair beside her, caught the edge instead of the center as he sat, and nearly tipped over.

"Sorry," he said.

"Michael," she laughed. "You're drunk!"

"It does seem that way," he said slowly.

"It's okay. It's a wedding. You're *supposed* to let go, have fun."

Nick went swinging by with the plain girl, who no longer seemed very plain at all. He gave Linda a little wave and did a flashy turn as he passed them.

Linda watched him dance off, her eyes soft.

"I guess you really like Nick a lot," Michael said.

Linda turned back to him. "Yes. I do."

Michael looked as if he were going to speak, but didn't.

The food ran out, but the drink and the music and the hilarity continued. Men went wobbling at intervals out into the abating storm to catch a breath of fresh air and expose themselves to the cold in the doomed hope that it would sober them up so they could start all over again. Now and then one was dragged or carried by his friends into one of the little conference rooms off the main hall and plopped on the carpeted floors to sleep it off. Young couples went hand-in-hand into the dim vestibule and squeezed in among the coats to kiss and touch each other and breathe in hoarse rasps.

A young Special Forces sergeant in razor-sharp dress uniform and highly polished jump boots entered the hall; a row of battle ribbons was pinned to his chest. He gave a curt nod to someone he knew, then went directly to the beer cooler, fished out a can, and sat down at one end of a debris-littered table, looking out at the people around him with an impassive face.

Axel's Tarzan yell rose loudly above the music. He stopped in the middle of the dance floor, took hold of the bridesmaid, who was his partner, by her shoulder and with a great *"Waugh!"* lifted her above his head to the full extension of his arms.

She batted at her dress, trying to remain modest, and swatted at him with her other hand. "Axel, what are you doing! Axel! You don't put me down, I'm gonna brain you! I swear!"

"I'm gonna kiss you!" Axel announced. "You gotta fuck or fight!"

There was general laughter around them.

Stan, who was standing across the room with John, paid no attention to Axel. He was staring at a handsome man with thickly waved hair who was dancing with his girl.

"Do you know what that son of a bitch is doing?" Stan said furiously. "That bastard is squeezing her ass!"

"Aw, it's only a wedding, Stanley."

Stan's lips pulled back from his teeth. "What do you mean, only a wedding? The guy is actually— There! Look! He did it again! Johnny, I'm gonna get my gun out of my coat. I'm gonna kill him! I'm gonna kill him right now!"

John reached for his shoulder. "Come on, Stanley."

Stan twisted out from under John's hand. To John's relief, he did not head toward the coats, but went instead to the dance floor and directly to his girl and her partner. He tapped the man's shoulder.

The man smiled, let go of the girl, and stood back. The girl canted out a hip, smirked, and waited. Stan threw a left hook that caught her on the side of the jaw and dropped her to the floor like a flour sack.

The man who had been dancing with her left the area immediately.

Stan stood looking about with his chin thrust out. Then he patted back the few strands of his hair that had come out of place when he'd swung.

Near the beer, clustered beside a pillar, Nick, Steven, and Michael stood together looking surreptitiously at the Special Forces sergeant.

"He just came back from there," Michael said.

"Yeah."

"He looks tough," Michael said. "Like a good killer. See that ribbon on the left? That's Quan Son."

"Boy," Steve said. "Boy."

"Come on along," Michael said.

He led the other two over to the sergeant.

"Hi. We, uh, we're going Airborne."

The sergeant looked up. He gave them a wide, blank smile. "Fuckit!"

"What?" Michael said.

The sergeant kept smiling.

Michael turned to Nick. "What'd he say?"

"Fuckit."

"Fuckit?"

"Fuckit," Nick confirmed.

"That's what I thought he said."

Steven nodded.

Michael cleared his throat. "Well, maybe you could tell us how it is over there."

"Fuckit," the sergeant said.

Michael looked at Nick. Nick looked at Steven. Steven looked at Michael. All three of them laughed, uneasily.

"Yeah, well, thanks a lot," Michael said.

"Don't mention it."

They walked away until they had put several people between themselves and the sergeant. Then they broke into laughter.

"Too much!" said Nick.

Axel came up to them. Sweat was pouring down his face. His jacket was split up the back. He jerked his thumb at the sergeant. "Who the hell is that guy?"

"Who the hell knows?" Michael said.

"Is he from around here?"

"Hell, no."

"Well, where's he from, then?"

In unison, Michael and Steven said, "Who the hell knows?"

Verging on sobriety, Michael said, "Maybe he's lost."

"Fuckin' A!" said Axel.

"Everybody's getting around the stage," Nick said. "I think Angela and Steven are going to do something."

Almost everyone was drunk. They were all talking and joking and pushing at one another and pulling streamers and bags of rice from their pockets. Angela and Steven mounted the stage. There was rowdy cheering, and a barrage of lewd shouts. Angela lifted her bouquet. The band's drummer struck up a roll. Angela tossed the bouquet high. It sailed through the air, accompanied by the drum roll, and fell into Linda's hands. The drummer struck his cymbals when she caught it.

Steven's mother got up onto the stage. She held two long-stemmed glasses filled with wine. She offered one to each of them.

"If you don't spill any," she said, "it's good luck for the rest of your lives."

Steven and Angela lifted the glasses and drank.

In the crowd, Nick turned to Linda and said suddenly, "Will you marry me?"

Linda flushed. She stared down at the bouquet. After several minutes she looked back up and said, "Okay."

"What?"

Linda nodded solemnly.

"You would?" he said, stunned as much by his having asked as by her answer. "What I mean is, if we get back from . . . I mean, *when* we get back." He shook his head. "I don't know what the hell I mean."

"I guess what goes through your mind comes out

your mouth," she said sadly. Her eyes moistened. Her lip began to tremble.

"You really would?"

"Really," she said.

Nick stared at her. "Terrific!"

"It is terrific!" she affirmed.

Linda dropped the bouquet and threw her arms around Nick.

"I don't know what we've been waiting for!" she said.

"I don't know. I don't know, either."

He kissed her, then hugged her tightly, threw back his head, and laughed.

He saw a drop of wine fall from the edge of Angela's upraised glass to stain the white of her wedding gown.

Chapter 5

Michael stood with the others outside the door of the VFW hall. All that remained of the storm was a light powder that seemed to drift down in slow motion.

Steven and Angela were running toward Michael's Cadillac. A huge string of tin cans had been tied to the rear bumper. People were pursuing them, throwing rice and streamers.

Michael's tuxedo was stained. The lapel had been torn. His carnation was squashed and his clip-on bow tie dangled askew from the open collar of his shirt. The others had fared no better, except for Stan, who—tux impeccable, hair perfectly in place, and shoes still shined to a high gloss—looked as if he'd just stepped out of a fashion page. They were all drunk, but, incredibly, still popping the tops of cans, guzzling the beer down, and tossing the empties aside.

"Bullshit. That's bullshit," Michael said to Stan, with some temper.

"You wanna bet?"

"That's bullshit," Michael repeated, his fogged brain incapable of summoning anything new to say. "You're full o' bullshit."

"How much?" Stan said hotly. "How much do you wanna bet? Put your money where your mouth is."

"Go fuck yourself, Stan," Michael said.

Nick and Axel detached themselves from the group and plowed through the snow to intercept Steven. As Angela slid into the passenger seat, Nick and Axel grabbed up Steven, lifted him from the ground and carried him around to the driver's door, opened it, and tossed him behind the wheel.

Nick leaned into the car. Angela had her window rolled down and was shouting to someone outside.

"Don't worry about what Stan says," Nick whispered to Steven.

"Right." Steven nodded drunkenly.

"Just forget it. Forget what Stan says. He's got a big mouth."

Steven put his head close to Nick. Almost inaudibly, he said, "You know, I never really done it to Angela, Nicky."

"Great. That's great."

"No, I mean it. That's my one true secret in life, Nick."

Nick coughed to cover his astonishment. Then he said, "It's nothing, man. It's nothing. Just . . . forget about it."

Angela was still waving and calling to people outside the car.

"But what about having a kid?" Steven said. "What do I do when she has it?"

"That's Angela's part. Leave all that to her. Everybody has kids and no one thinks there's anything funny about it. Hang loose."

"Hang loose?"

Nick gave Steven a big hug. "Just hang loose!"

Steven nodded, staring out the windshield.

"Hey," Nick said. "Don't look so sad. Don't worry. Everything's gonna be great. See you Monday on the train."

"Right. See you Monday." He tapped Angela on the shoulder. "All set, babe?"

She nodded excitedly.

Steven put the car in gear and started off. People trotted alongside it, yelling and pounding on the top.

Suddenly, Michael burst out of the shadows and into the bright cones of the headlights. He was stark naked, and trailing a bunch of streamers from his upraised hand. He jumped up and down in the snow. Steven and Angela gaped, then laughed. Steven laid on the horn. Michael turned, presenting them his backside, and took off running, leading the car, the streamers flowing out behind him. He leaped and bounded, as if in the possession of a god, as if trying to break the restraints of gravity and soar up into pure, ethereal space.

Holding Michael's clothes, Axel watched him, his head bobbing. "Fuckin' A," he said to himself.

"All right, Steve!" John Welch belowed. "All right, Angela!"

The groom's friends set off after the car. Axel made

it only fifty yards, then he slipped on the slush and went down head over heels, scattering Michael's clothes.

Michael went leaping and running ahead of the Caddy, his skin bright white in the glare of the lights. Several hundred feet from the VFW hall the road forked, the left branch angling up a hill, the right turning down toward the town and Steven's mother's house, and the hulking mill, flames spurting from its tall stacks into the night.

Michael veered left, up the hill, toward a potholed old basketball court on a bluff that overlooked the valley. The Caddy turned right, and in moments the taillights disappeared behind a bend.

Some distance behind, Stan, Nick, and John came stumbling and panting. They turned up the hill after Michael.

Halfway up, John groaned and staggered over to a tree and leaned against it, waving Nick and Stan on with a gesture of surrender. Stan slowed and came to a halt a few yards farther on, stood catching his breath a moment, then frowned at the snow and slush covering his shoes, and began to pick it off with his fingers.

Nick was holding his side and gasping by the time he reached the court. He didn't see Michael.

Far below, the blast furnaces from the mill lit up the valley with an eerie light. Dogs from various houses were howling and barking.

"Michael?"

There was movement on the ground beneath the basket at the far end of the court. Nick walked over.

Michael was lying on his stomach in the slush, arms

and legs spread out. He rolled over as Nick approached.

"I must be out of my fucking mind. At my age. It's all moving too fast." He pulled himself to a sitting position, looked down into the valley, and was quiet for several moments. "You think we'll ever come back?"

Abrupt fear lanced through Nick. "From 'Nam?"

"Yeah," Michael said.

Nick didn't answer, couldn't find any words. He extended a hand and helped Michael to his feet. He slipped out of his tuxedo jacket and draped it around Michael's shoulders. Michael was shivering. They stood together, looking down at the glow of the blast furnaces.

"You know something?" Nick said, shattering their reverie. "The whole thing is right here. I love this fuckin' place. I know that sounds crazy, but if anything happens, Mike, don't leave me over there. I mean, don't leave me. You gotta promise me, Mike."

Pulling the jacket tighter around himself, Michael gave a half laugh. "Nick—"

"You gotta promise," Nick said urgently. "You got to!"

"Hey, you got it, pal!"

Tension left Nick's body. He laughed loudly. "Let's go huntin'!" he said. "Right now. Let's keep moving until we have to get on that train to Dix. Let's not stop for anything!"

Michael was driving. They'd rounded up John, Axel, and Stan, and picked up Michael's Caddy. They were an hour out of town already, still in their soiled tuxes, jammed in amid knapsacks and sleeping bags, rifles, and cases of beer. They were popping the tops of cans and passing them back and forth.

"Down from heaven—" Michael sang.

Nick joined him: "—came eleven, shout Geronimo!"

"What the hell is that?" said Stan.

"The screamin' Eagles Airborne Song!"

"The screamin' assholes," Stan said.

Axel said, "Fuckin' A!" He started his own song. "Let me be free! Let me be free! If . . . you . . . will let me be free . . . You'll always be happy . . . with me-eeeeee."

John put his hands to his mouth and made a trumpet's sound. "Wa-wa-wa! Waaaaa!"

The sky began to lighten. Michael was blinking and nodding. He pulled to the side of the road and turned the wheel over to Nick. He was asleep in minutes.

The Caddy forged on, tires hissing against the new snow, feathery plumes of powder trailing out behind them.

John went to sleep in the rear seat. Axel and Stan stared out the windows.

Nick drove on, yawning, shaking his head now and then, and blinking.

"You know," Stan said to Axel, "I got it on with Angela."

"She fucked you?" Axel said.

"Yeah. At Billy's party. We did it in Steve's car out in the garage."

Axel's face became solemn. "She fucked me, too."

"She fucked you?" Stan said, appalled.

"Fuckin' A."

There was silence a while.

"Steve don't know she fucked us both," Stan said.

"Yeah."

"Maybe it's one of our kids. Fucking women, they're all alike."

Axel nodded slowly, as if assimilating this thought. "Fuckin' A," he said.

The night disappeared by degrees, and a gray dawn came. Everyone was awake now, but no one was talking, all of them hung over and blunted.

"Holy shit!" Nick said, snapping suddenly alert at the wheel.

He slammed his foot against the brake pedal. The car slid sideways, bumped a rear fender against a snowbank, spun around in a circle, and came to a stop. The passengers were thrown up against each other.

Standing immobile in the center of the road, staring at them, was a young dun buck with four points on his antlers.

"Son of a bitch!" Stan said. "Get him! For Christ's sake, somebody get him!"

"Who's got the ammo?" John said, feverishly working the bolt of his rifle.

"Ammo! Get ammo!" Axel said.

Stan was pawing through the backpacks. "I'll get it! Where is it?"

Michael sat, quiet and unperturbed, in the front seat, gazing out at the buck, as the others searched frantically for ammunition.

"It's in the trunk!" John said.

"No, it's not."

"It's in the trunk, Axel! It's in the trunk! I'm telling you, it's in the trunk!"

Stan, Axel, and John piled out through the rear doors. Axel began kicking at the trunk.

"Goddamn it, hurry up, my gun's in there!" Stan screamed.

"Get me some fuckin' ammo!" John said.

Nick sat still in the front seat with Michael. They turned from the deer to look at each other. Michael picked up his rifle, which was resting against the seat between him and Nick. He opened the door and got out. He looked back at the commotion around the trunk. His mouth turned down in disgust.

The deer was still in the center of the road, mesmerized by the headlights.

"Get out of here!" Michael yelled angrily. "Damn you, get out. Go home! . . . Scat! . . . Shoo!"

The deer blinked.

He heard the sound of the trunk popping open.

"Give me those fuckin' bullets!" Stan said.

"Go on, scat!" Michael yelled. He jacked a shell into the chamber of his rifle, put the but to his shoulder, and blasted the round over the deer's head.

The deer bolted away in panic.

"Get lost!" Michael yelled after it.

Stan and Axel and John came running up to him, loaded rifles in their hands. They looked after the deer in puzzlement.

"Jesus," Stan said. "You're still goddamn drunk. The point is to shoot the bastards, not chase 'em away."

Chapter 6

The Caddy moved slowly up a narrow road flanked on both sides by pine-forested ridges. The branches of the pines were festooned with snow and they drooped under the weight. The snowfall had stopped, but there were still dark, wind-driven clouds moving across the sky. Above the rim of the mountains, on the eastern horizon, was a soft, pink glow.

Stan was leaning over the front seat, watching the road. He had a can of beer in his hand. "Here!" he said. He pointed, and beer slopped out of the can onto Nick.

"Watch it, dickhead!"

Stan pounded Nick on the shoulder. "Here! This is it. This is the place we stopped at last year."

"It is not," Axel said.

John hunched his head forward and peered out through the windshield. "It's up ahead, Stan."

"There's no way it's up ahead," Stan said indignantly. "I tell you, this is it."

No one said anything more. Nick kept driving. Stan sat back sulkily, drained his beer, and opened another one. Nick drove on for another quarter-hour.

"I think this is it," he said, as they came abreast of a lightning-blasted tree. He pulled to the side of the road and set the handbrake.

"This is not it! Definitely!" Stan said. "This is not it, or else they changed it somehow."

"Why the hell would they do that? And who? And how?" Michael said.

"Goddamn it, this is not it! And I want to go where we went last year!"

Axel said, "You're full of shit, Stanley."

Stan spun around. *"Who'd* you say was full of shit?"

"You're full of shit. You're always full of shit."

Stan glared at Axel. Axel's mouth thinned out. After a moment, Stan looked away and coughed.

"Holy shit," he said. "I'm starving."

"Break out the food," Stan said.

John rummaged through the clutter in the back seat and came up with a paper bag. He pulled out plastic-wrapped packages of bologna slices, a jar of mustard, a couple of small bags of potato chips, and some packaged sweets. He passed them out. Everyone but Nick began to eat, tearing open the packages, dipping slices of bologna into the mustard, cramming potato chips into their mouths. They opened more beer.

Axel was chewing bologna and potato chips together. Tiny crumbs fell from his mouth. "Let me ask you a question, Nicky. How come I never see you eat anything?"

"Sometimes I like to starve myself—keeps the fear up."

"It ain't natural," Axel said. "What do you say, John?"

"I don't know. Hey, that bologna's mine, Axel."

Axel was pulling another package out of the bag. "You want it?"

"Damn right."

"Mike," Axel said, "are you gonna eat that Twinkie?"

Michael handed the Twinkie back over the seat to Axel. "Here."

"Thanks." Axel tore off the wrapper, dipped the Twinkie into the mustard jar, and stuffed it into his mouth.

"That's mustard!" John said with disbelief.

"What?" Axel said, chewing.

"You just put mustard on your Twinkie."

"So what? Jesus, you sound like a traffic cop. Gimme another beer."

John passed a can over, shaking his head.

Stan was scowling out the window. "Definitely. This is not it! I'm telling you, they changed it."

Axel said, "You can't find your own ass with two hands."

Stan began a retort, thought better of it, and said, "Jesus, it's freezing."

John banged his forehead with his hand. "You know, we forgot to make a toast to Steven and Angela."

Stan shrugged. No one said anything.

Michael wiped his mouth. "Well, if we're going to go hunting, let's go."

They finished off their beers and got out. Alex kicked the trunk and it popped open. The pink dawn had been short-lived. The sky was a dull, soiled gray above the dark clouds again, and the wind funneling through the valley was cold. It nipped at their ruined tuxedoes. They opened their packs and laid out their gear, draped it over the fenders, piled it on the seats, and began changing.

"Wheee-uuh!" John said, naked except for his shorts, and hurrying to pull on his long johns.

Nick hugged himself. "Jesus! It's really *freezing.*"

"Fuckin' A!"

Stan said, "You know, you got a really terrific vocabulary, Axel."

"Fuckin' A!"

"Mikey," Stan said, "hey, Mikey, you got any extra thermal socks?"

Michael was in his hunting gear already. He was several paces away from the car, hunkered down, studying the terrain of the mountainside that rose above them. He looked over.

Stan was digging into the chaos of his pack. "Oops. Never mind, Mike. Never mind. I got 'em. . . . Where the hell are my boots? Anyone see my boots?" He pawed through the trunk. "Who the hell took my boots?"

He went to the back seat of the car, began rummaging through it, tossing empty bologna packs, beer cans, shoving everyone else's gear around.

"Watch it, dickhead!"

"Hey, Stan, that's my shirt you just dropped in the snow."

"Somebody took my boots," Stan complained. "I bought 'em special. I know I put my special boots in here."

He ransacked the car, went back to the trunk, searched through it again.

"All right," he said. He put his hands on his hips and looked around accusingly. "All right, you guys. Whoever took my boots, I want 'em back!" He was still in his dress pants and good shoes. On his torso he wore a red, oversized down vest, which he'd borrowed from Axel.

The others were all in their gear. They looked at him with annoyance. This same scene had been played several times before.

"I got a boot for you, Stan." Axel lifted his foot as if preparing to kick. "Here, right up your ass."

Stan danced away. He spied Michael's pack, picked it up, and looked inside. "Hey, Mikey, you got your spares along. Lemme borrow 'em."

"No," Michael said quietly.

"No?"

"No."

Stan took the boots out and turned them over in his hands. "What do you mean, no?"

"What I mean by no, Stan, is *no*."

Stan dropped the boots down on top of the pack. "Some fuckin' friend," he said sourly. "You're some fuckin' friend, Mike."

Michael came over and put his extra boots back in his pack. "You gotta learn, Stan. Every goddamn year you come up here with your head up your ass—"

"Maybe the view looks better to him from up there," Axel interjected.

There were laughs.

"You got no jacket," Michael said. "You got no pants, you got no knife, and you got no boots. All you got is that stupid pistol you carry around like some wiseguy cop. You think that's always gonna take care of you. That's what you think. That's all you think."

"Aw, what the hell," Axel said. "Give him the boots, Mike."

"No. No boots. No nothin'. Not any more."

Stan thrust out his jaw. "You're a fuckin' bastard, Mike. You know that? You're a miserable fuckin' selfish bastard!"

Michael rose. He jabbed his finger down at the ground. "*This* is *this,* Stan. This isn't something else. *This* is *this!* This time you're on your own."

"I fixed you up a million times, Mike!" Stan stomped over to the others and addressed them. "I fixed him up a million times. I don't know how many times I fixed him up with girls and nothing ever happens. Zero, that's all. A big zero!"

"Come on, Stan," Axel said.

Stan turned and pointed a finger. "The trouble with you, Mike, is that no one ever knows what the hell you're talkin' about! *'This* is *this.'* What does all that bullshit mean, *'This* is *this?'* "

He faced the others again. "I mean, is that some faggot-sounding bullshit he's running down, or is that some faggot-sounding bullshit! And if it isn't, then what the hell is it?"

They shifted in embarrassment.

Stan spun back to Michael. "You know what I think? There's times I swear I think you're a goddamn faggot!"

John said, "Hey, Stan. Cut it out."

Stan banged a fist into his palm. "Last week! Just last week he could o' had that new redhead waitress at the Bowladrome. He could o' had it knocked. And look what he did. I mean, look what he fuckin' did. Nothin'! That's what!"

"Stan!" John snapped with uncharacteristic anger. "Shut the hell up!"

Michael was staring at Stan. His face was expressionless, but his eyes were hard and bright. His gaze didn't waver.

Nick watched Michael closely.

The others began to shift under the tension.

John waved a big hand. "Oh, hell. I'll give you my boots, Stan. I'll stay in the car and listen to the radio."

Michael worked the bolt of his rifle, chambering a cartridge. "I said *no."*

His voice cracked like a whiplash in the stillness of the mountain dawn.

John went rigid. The color drained from his face.

He glanced at Axel, who was standing behind him, then both men stepped back, out of the way.

Stan and Michael faced each other. Stan's shoulders twitched. His mouth fell open, closed, then opened again. He breathed through it. His hand began edging toward his jacket pocket, where his pistol lay. Michael's eyes didn't leave his.

Nick stepped between them. He said nothing. He looked quietly and hard into Michael's face. Then he bent down, pulled Michael's spare boots from the knapsack, walked over to Stan and threw them down in front of Stan's feet.

Stan laughed. His shoulders loosened. His hand fell away from his pocket. He laughed again.

No one else did.

The dull sun was a quarter of the way up the sky. The wind kicked up swirls and clouds of fine, powdery snow from the high slope, and went keening through the trees.

Michael was a dozen paces to the side and a little ahead of Nick. He moved with patient care, advancing a step, freezing for several moments to scan the tree-line and listen, then advancing another step.

The snow was shin-deep here, but they'd had to bull through drifts on their climb, and snow was crusted on their pants nearly to their waists. Nick was bone-weary and short of breath, but he forced himself to keep pace with Michael and to keep from gasping, which could panic a skittish deer.

Michael froze in mid-step, his right foot suspended an inch above the snow.

Nick went rigid, his senses suddenly tuned and searching.

He heard a faint crack—a small branch breaking.

Almost imperceptibly, Michael lowered his foot, set his weight. With agonizing slowness, he lifted his rifle to his shoulder.

Nick followed the direction of Michael's gaze, trying to see something in the treeline. He couldn't.

He saw Michael flick his safety off, with the tiniest twitch of his finger.

Then, as if by magic, a large, black-muzzled, broad-shouldered buck appeared, stepping over a snow-encrusted deadfall. It was a princely animal, mythic against the backdrop of snow and pine and mountainside. It lifted its head to test the air.

The shot exploded. A thin lance of pale flame and a small puff of white smoke exploded from the muzzle of Michael's rifle.

The deer sprang straight up in the air, spun around, then dropped in its tracks. A foreleg twitched once, and then it was still.

Michael turned. He looked at Nick. They stood a moment in frozen tableau. Then Michael shrugged out of his pack. He opened it and took a length of rope from it, a dragline. He set his rifle carefully on top of the pack, out of the snow. He drew out the gutting knife sheathed at his hip, and walked through the snow toward the deer.

Nick followed.

* * *

They drapped the deer down to the old logger's shack they had used last year as a base camp, about a third of a mile above the road, and hung it up in a tree, to keep skunks and coons away from it.

They had called out to the camp when they'd caught sight of it, but although there were footprints in the snow all around it, no one had answered.

With the deer hanging, they pushed open the door and went inside. It was a small, ruined building, about nine by twelve feet. The floor had rotted out long ago, boards were missing from the walls, and the entire structure leaned sharply toward the downward slope. An unlit Coleman lantern hung from a rafter, swaying in the wind. Slats of light cut through the openings in the walls.

Stan, Axel, and John were all asleep in their sleeping bags, amid a litter of beer cans. Snow swirled through the cracks and had drifted over them. The wind gusted and moaned.

"I guess they didn't get anything," Nick said.

"Are you surprised?" Michael asked.

They broke out their own sleeping bags and unrolled them. Michael scrounged up a couple of cans of beer that had not been opened. They sat down on their gear and drank.

"Tomorrow," Michael said. "Tomorrow I'll take Stan out with me."

"You? Hunt with Stan?"

Michael tossed his head. "Yeah. I mean, he doesn't know anything about anything. He's just a bullshit with angel's wings. What the hell."

A wind topped the mountain above them and came roaring down the slope. It struck the cabin like a fist, making it shudder.

The Sunday night traffic on the highway running past Clairton was heavy, an unbroken river of cars. Michael weaved in and out, laying on the horn for the tight squeezes, which were many. The gutted deer was lashed across the driver's fender, frozen stiff, the rope-ends flapping against the car.

Inside, the hunters were guzzling beer, bullshitting, telling jokes, and whooping with laughter.

Michael cut in front of a van, ignoring the angry blare of its horn, and whipped the Caddy onto the off-ramp for Clairton. He circled on the underpass and came out onto Division Street, glancing for a moment at the fire-bright sprawl of the mill, then went on, toward Steven's house.

When they reached it, he pulled up to the curb and blasted the horn. Axel and Stan rolled down the rear windows and pulled themselves partway out of the car, banged against the doors and the roof, whistled and shouted for Steven and Angela. Michael sounded a tattoo on the horn. Neighborhood dogs began to bark. Figures appeared in windows of nearby houses.

A window on the second floor opened. Steven leaned out and waved.

"Hey, Steve!" Axel bellowed. "What'd'ya say! Piece o' fuckin' cake!"

Between Axel and Stan on the rear seat, John Welch said, "Hey, let's go to my place and have a nightcap."

"All right!"

"Fuckin' A!"

"Let's go."

Michael put the car in gear and pulled away with a spray of slush.

There were half a dozen open bottles on the bar. Only a few of the lights were on. The hunters sat around a table with glasses before them, quiet and subdued, beyond the point of exhaustion.

"I don't goddamn believe it," Stan said, his bloodshot eyes half closed. "But I don't think I can drink one more drop of anything. Even water."

By their silence, the others agreed with him.

From outside, they could hear the clanks and bangings and whistles from the mill.

Michael was at the door, absorbed in the sound.

Abruptly, John got up. He went over to the piano and raised the cover from the keyboard. He sat down and put his fingers on the keys.

He began to play a Chopin nocturne. It was nothing that the others could recognize, but they were all affected by the soft, haunting, melancholic strains, and they turned to him and watched him in silence.

John's eyes were closed. He swayed almost imperceptibly on the bench with the music.

There came the noise of an approaching train along the tracks that ran behind the bar. It became louder, momentarily drowning out the music, and then the train passed by with a roar, shaking the building and rattling glasses on the shelves. Then it was gone, leaving the music clear and dominant once again.

Michael and Nick looked at each other. The corners of Michael's mouth moved up in his spare, enigmatic smile. He closed his eyes and leaned back in his chair, listening to John play.

Book Two

THE JUNGLE
1970

Chapter 1

Lush, forested mountains rose up around the small valley on all four sides. The sun was a blinding disc high up in the sky, and the heat was a smothering blanket.

A dirt road led to a cluster of grass huts in the center of the valley. Scattered across the road, around the craters of exploded mortar rounds, were the bodies of a platoon of American Rangers. They lay sprawled and twisted, some without limbs, a couple with ropes of intestines uncoiled beside them. Dark blood stained their uniforms and had soaked into the dirt. Flies buzzed over the corpses, and a mangy brown dog lapped at one of the pools of blood. There was silence in the thick, humid air.

Faintly, there came the sound of an approaching helicopter.

It became louder, a roar, then the gunship flashed

around an outcropping of rock at the notch through which the road ran, came streaking low over the jumbled corpses, and drove straight for the village.

Long, slender rockets racked on the helicopter's belly streaked away with thin trails of flame and smoke. They lanced into the village.

A line of explosions tore huts apart, sent burning pieces spinning high into the air.

The helicopter shot upward, passed over the wreckage of the village, then soared out through the notch at the other end of the village, and was gone.

From the thick, vine-roped jungle to the east of the village, a single figure in black pants and black shirt appeared, carrying a Russian AK-47 assault rifle. He advanced warily, paused, studied the corpses of the Rangers, swept his eyes over the tilled fields to the west, then looked to the burning village.

He raised a hand. A squad of Viet Cong detached themselves from the jungle, spread out, and began to advance through the tall grass.

A hundred yards to the side of them, one of the fallen Rangers twitched. His eyelids snapped open. His clear, crazed eyes darted over the fat clouds drifting above him. There was a deep, clotted gash across his forehead. The blood had run down his face into his beard, encrusting and stiffening it.

A hand grenade exploded.

Michael jerked, then forced himself to lie still. With excruciating slowness, he shifted his head until he was looking in the direction from which the explosion had come.

The VC were gathered around a smoking pit, jabbering. Several of the villagers had been hiding there, beneath camouflage of bamboo poles and fern branches. Three of them—all that had survived the grenade blast—came staggering up and out. One, a woman, held a bloodied baby in her hands. One of the VCs trained his weapon on them and cut loose with automatic fire. The villagers were stitched across their torsos and flung back down into the pit.

The VCs were standing around the smoking pit, pointing in and speaking excitedly among themselves.

Michael pulled himself to his hands and feet, groaning, and crawled to a dead Ranger a few feet away. With shaking hands, he stripped the flamethrower from the dead man's back. He dragged it off to the side of the road, behind a clump of bushes, and laboriously, painfully, worked the harness up over his shoulders. His expression was detached, dreamlike.

He waited, the madness gone from his eyes, but nothing else having replaced it. They were clear—and empty.

The VC, about a dozen of them, approached the dead Rangers. Their attitude was more relaxed, growing casual, even. They held their weapons loosely; a couple of them joked.

They gathered around the corpses, slung their weapons across their backs or laid them aside, and began stripping watches and rings from the dead Americans, turning out pockets.

In one motion, Michael stood, depressed the stud on the nozzle of the flame thrower, and stepped around the bushes with the flamethrower on full burn, sweeping the long broad line of jellied fire across the enemy soldiers.

Their high screams were lost in the roar of the jetting flame. Their clothes and hair burst into fire, fire clung to their thrashing limbs, fire enveloped their fallen twisting bodies, fire covered and obliterated them. A great coil of greasy, black smoke rose from the holocaust. Michael advanced step by step, burning them, his eyes vacant.

When he released the stud, ending the flame, the VC were crumpled in a ragged circle, humped and grotesque, smoldering, charred, tiny yellow flames flickering here and there.

From somewhere in the fields to the west, more villagers materialized, huddling together and pointing at Michael, who stood with legs braced apart, smoke curling up from the fabric of his pants and shirt.

He did not turn as a Huey broke through the notch behind him, hovered over the road, then settled in a cloud of dust.

The chopper remained on the ground only seconds, just long enough for a platoon of support Rangers, too late, to leap out and deploy, crouching as they ran beneath the downdraft of the whirling rotors. Then it lifted off again, and soared away.

The lieutenant leading them came running up behind Michael. Michael whirled suddenly, his finger on the nozzle stud. The lieutenant snapped his AR-15 to his shoulder. They stood frozen a moment, then each lowered his weapon.

"What the hell happened?" the lieutenant said.

Michael looked at him a moment. Then he said, "Fuckit."

Spread in a wide line, the Rangers stopped behind the lieutenant. He stepped toward the village, and waved them on.

"Move it out, mudfuckers! Move it out!"

Michael stood still, gazing at the far sky as the Rangers passed, their eyes pausing on him a second, then flicking forward again.

One of them stopped and gasped. "Michael? Jesus, Michael!"

Michael looked at him dumbly.

"Michael, for Christ's sake, it's me, Steven!"

Steven threw his arms around Michael and hugged him fiercely.

"Nick!" he shouted. "Come here, come here! It's Michael!"

One of the Rangers who had passed turned and came running back. He came to a skidding halt and gaped.

"Michael! Oh my God!"

Automatic rifle fire ripped from the treeline. The lieutenant and two other Rangers crumpled to the ground.

A line of exploding mortar shells walked down the side of the road, hurling soldiers into the air and dumping them back to the ground like broken dolls.

Nick lunged, hit Michael, and drove him to the earth. "Get down!" he screamed.

The mortar barrage ended, there was a moment of eerie stillness, then a horde of VCs erupted from the jungle toward the Rangers, screaming and firing on the run. . . .

* * *

A large, gray heron walked with slow steps in the shallows of the wide river, rain falling around it, and stopped now and then to cock its head and stare into the water, then plunged its bill down to come up with a wriggling silver minnow. It arched its neck back and swallowed the minnow whole.

High mountain peaks towered above the river. A little way up the sandy strip of beach was a grass fishing hut, one end resting on an incline of land, the other supported by pilings to which rolls of barbed concertina wire had been nailed, making a kind of cage. There were several shadowy figures contained within this cage.

A VC soldier came out of the hut, walked down the incline and past the caged men without glancing at them, and strode a dozen paces farther, close to the edge of the river. A pit had been dug into the sand there, and roofed over with a stout bamboo grating that was held down with heavy stones. There was a handful of men in the pit, South Vietnamese and American soldiers. The river was rising and water was spilling in, already up to the chests and shoulders of some of the trapped men.

The VC stood at the edge of the grating and looked down. The prisoners regarded him without a sound. Then one began to babble. He thrust pleading hands up through the grate. The VC opened his pants, took out his penis, and urinated onto the trapped men. He finished, shook his penis, put it away, then turned and walked back to the hut.

The hut was a single room, about fifteen feet square. There were woven sleeping pallets on the floor, and weapons, equipment, and meager food stores on the floor along the walls, but the only piece of furniture was a tin kitchen table with a plastic top and two chairs, one on either side.

Seated in the chairs, facing each other, were two South Vietnamese prisoners. Their faces were bruised and their eyes frightened. One was barely out of his teens. The other, in his late twenties, was trembling violently. A VC officer stood beside them, shouting in rapid, angry Vietnamese. There were half a dozen other VC in the hut, chattering volubly and shaking piaster notes and American currency at each other, waving stolen watches.

The officer menaced the South Vietnamese with his rifle barrel, snapping out something harsh and threatening. Shakily, they picked up the strips of red rag he had thrown on the table and tied them around their heads. Between them lay a captured Colt Python .357 Magnum with a double American Eagle carved into its ivory grip.

When the rags were in place the officer took up the revolver, swung out the cylinder and slid a single, stubby, hollow-nosed cartridge into one chamber. He snapped the cylinder closed and spun it around. He smiled at the prisoners.

Swigging from cans of captured American beer, the VC watched, their excitement escalating.

Below, looking up through the interstices in the floor boards, was a handful of South Vietnamese and American prisoners, caged within the barbed wire around the hut's pilings. They were bruised and cut, haggard, filthy, and their elbows were tied behind their backs.

The VC placed the last of their bets, and grew quiet.

The officer cocked the revolver. He pointed the muzzle up at the roof, hesitated, then pulled the trigger.

The gun went off with a deafening explosion. The big slug tore a hole through the roof, and pieces of thatched straw came fluttering down.

The South Vietnamese at the table winced.

The officer loaded another cartridge into the Magnum, spun the cylinder again, then placed it on the table between the seated prisoners. He gave the gun a twirl. It turned a couple of revolutions, then came to a stop. The barrel pointed to the younger prisoner. He ran his tongue over his lips, then snatched the gun up, cocked it, pressed it to his temple, and pulled the trigger. The hammer fell on an empty chamber.

The officer took the gun, replaced it on the table and shoved it toward the older prisoner. The man was shaking uncontrollably. He raised the gun with a trembling hand, spun the cylinder, put the barrel to his head, cocked the hammer, moaned, and closed his eyes. He pulled the trigger. The hammer clicked on nothing.

There were hoots from the VC.

The officer took the gun, spun the cylinder, cocked the weapon, put the muzzle up to the boy's temple and pulled the trigger himself. Nothing happened. He passed the gun back to the older prisoner.

This time the man took it up with giddy confidence.

He prepared the gun, put it to his head, squeezed the trigger.

The Magnum went off. It blew the prisoner's head apart, hammered him out of his chair and through the flimsy thatched wall to fall in a crumpled heap on the sand below.

Some of the VC jeered, others celebrated and collected their winnings.

Under the hut, Nick stifled a cry and turned away. Steven was sitting on his feet, looking out to the river, crying. Michael continued to stare up through the floorboards, noting every gesture, every motion of the VC. The tiniest smile flickered for an instant over his mouth, then disappeared.

There were five bodies with mutilated heads sprawled at the side of the fishing hut, three South Vietnamese and two Americans. Steven's legs buckled as two of the VC hauled him past the bodies up into the hut.

Michael was seated on one side of the table. His face was empty, but his mouth was set in a hard line. The guards pushed Steven into the chair across from him.

"Oh, God!" Steven said. He buried his face in his hands and began rocking back and forth.

The VC began a new, loud round of betting.

Michael reached across the Magnum that lay between them and touched Steven.

"You can do it," he said quietly.

Steven uncovered his face, stared at the pistol. "Oh,

shit. Oh, shit. I can't hack it, Mike." His voice was numb with terror.

"Steven. Listen to me, Steven! You have to do it."

Steven whimpered and curled in upon himself. His voice became thin, childlike. "I want to go home, Michael. We don't belong here in the jungle."

Michael banged a fist on the table. "Use your fucking head!"

Steven winced. "Oh, God. *This is horrible!*"

"Listen to me, Steven," Michael said urgently. "If you don't go through with it, they'll put you in the pit. You'll die—you understand? You'll die!"

Steven shook his head slowly, wonderingly. "We don't belong here in the jungle, Michael. I just wanna go home!"

Michael's voice became gentle. "Hey, listen, so do I."

Steven nodded.

"Believe me," Michael said. "You can do this. You can. If we *both* do it, then we all get to go home, see? You and me and Nicky."

The VC officer loaded the gun and spun it. Steven could see nothing else. The barrel pointed to him. He stared at it. Tears filled his eyes. He shook his head: *No.* The VC were yelling unintelligibly at him. Michael reached across, and clapping him on the shoulder, gave him a smile of unwavering faith.

"Go ahead," he said. "It'll be all right. I promise you."

Steven looked directly into Michael's eyes, draining Michael's strength to fill the hollowness of his own pulling fear. He picked up the gun, holding Michael's eyes with his own, fumbled the cylinder around, cocked the weapon, and held it to his head.

Michael gave him an encouraging nod. Steven began to squeeze the trigger—but at the last instant he jerked the gun aside.

The Magnum thundered. The grazing slug ripped open his scalp and the muzzle blast burned his skin.

Michael's face went dead.

Steven sat motionless, still holding the Colt, his mouth pursed in consummate puzzlement, blood running down the side of his face. He began to cry.

There were angry voices among the VC. One of them clubbed Steven in the chest with a rifle stock, knocking him out of the chair. He curled up in a little ball, sobbing. The officer muttered something in a disgusted tone. Two guards dragged Steven from the hut.

They returned with a South Vietnamese soldier who couldn't have been more than seventeen. They shoved him into the chair across from Michael. The boy looked at Michael in terror.

Chapter 2

The rain became a deluge in the late afternoon, and kept falling through the night and into the next morning. Cascades of water splashed down the incline, flooding the compound beneath the hut. Steven was lying on his side in the mud, knees tucked up to his chest, and arms wrapped around his knees. Michael had torn off one of his sleeves and bound Steven's head wound with it, but he could get no response from him. Steven stared straight ahead, his face frozen in horror.

Two Vietnamese crouched side by side in one corner, occasionally conversing in low, melancholic tones. Near them was the body of a third Vietnamese, who had died during the night of battle wounds.

Michael was standing ankle deep in muck and water at the front of the compound, looking at the pit.

Water from the flooding river was lapping at its

edge, gurgling into it, and rivulets of rain and runny mud were entering from the other side. Last night there had been four pairs of hands clinging to the bamboo grating. This morning there was only one pair —and the hands were slipping now, vanishing for a few moments, then clawing back up....

Nick was sitting against one of the pilings, careful of the barbs on the wire, picking at the threads around a tear in his pants at the knee.

Michael turned back to him, his face filled with exasperation.

"I'm telling you, Nick, it's up to us!"

"Who do you think you are, God?"

"What? Are you hoping?" Michael said angrily. "Praying? What?"

"Is there anything else"

"Yeah, I thought so. I thought you were praying. How bad do you want to get out of this, Nick?"

Nick gave him a sour look. "What do you think?"

"Then listen to me, damn it! We're outta options! This is no fucking time for hoping or praying or wishing or any other bullshit with angel's wings. This is *it. Here we are.* And we gotta get out!"

"You're right. Okay, you're right. You're always right! Okay?"

"Get off your fucking ass and stand up!" Nick looked away. Michael grabbed him and jerked him to his feet. "Get off your ass, Nick!"

"Okay, okay! I'm standing." Nick straightened his shoulders. "What about Steven?"

"Forget him."

Nick's eyes widened. "What the hell are you saying?"

"I'm saying forget about Steven. Steven ain't gonna make it, Nick."

"Forget about Steven?"

"Look in his eyes. There's nothing but snakes running around under his skin. He's in a dream and he won't come out."

"Mike—"

"Listen, Nick! Get it through your head or you and me are both dead, too!"

There was a shout from above in the hut. The two South Vietnamese jumped in fright. Through the spaces between the floorboards the VC could be seen, slugging from beer cans, challenging each other, pointing down at the floor. The officer was brandishing the Magnum like a prize.

Nick squinted up at them, chewing on his lower lip.

"Nick," Michael said, utterly calm. "We gotta play with more bullets."

Nick was incredulous. "What?"

"I'm gonna get more bullets into that gun, Nick. It's the only way."

"More bullets in the gun?"

"More bullets," Michael said flatly. "But the trouble is, that still leaves one of us down here, so that means we gotta play each other."

"More bullets? . . . Against each other? . . . Are you crazy?"

"It's the only choice we've got."

"It's a pretty shitty choice."

The legs of the guards appeared, coming down the incline. The rain was beginning to lighten.

"How many more bullets" Nick asked.

Michael looked at him carefully. "Three—minimum."

The guards were outside the barbed wire.

"No fucking way!"

Michael held him with his eyes. "I'll pick the moment, Nick. The game goes on until I move. When I start shooting, go for the nearest guard. Get his gun and zap the motherfucker."

"I'm not ready for this!"

Michael ignored him. "Whatever gun you get, zap the fuckers."

"You're crazy!" Nick shouted. "No way! You've gone completely insane!"

At Nick's shout, a guard fired off a burst that chopped splinters out of the piling behind him, a foot above his head. Nick and Michael jumped back. The guard gestured with his rifle, directing them to the far side of the compound. They moved.

The guards entered, grabbed Steven beneath his shoulders, and dragged him to the gate. Steven wouldn't stand. A guard smashed him in the kidney with a rifle butt. Steven shrieked in pain.

"You sonsabitches!" Nick jumped forward. Michael moved with him.

The other guards clubbed them to their knees.

Steven was hauled out and the gate was closed. Nick leaned against a piling for support, watching. Michael stood next to him. The guards brought Steven to the edge of the pit. He was on his feet now, pliable in their hands. He turned and looked back at the compound. His face was dreamy and distant.

"It's up to you, Nick," Michael said. "Now it's all up to you."

After a moment, Nick said, "Okay. I must be outta my fuckin' mind, but okay."

At the pit, the guards raised the bamboo grate. Steven looked in, then pulled violently back.

"They're all dead!" he screamed. "They're drowned. They're floating in there! No! No!"

The guards wrestled him forward and threw him in. Muddy water splashed out of the pit. They slammed the grate back down, replaced the anchoring stones.

Steven's hands appeared, groping frantically, clutching around the grate. "Oh, God!" he screamed.
"There's leeches in here. I'll die! Oh, God, God—*please!*"

The guards came walking back. The officer looked into the compound, eyes moving over each of the men there, the Magnum dangling from a finger.

"Now," Michael said. He slugged Nick in the stomach, kneed him in the chest as he went down.

"Him against me!" he screamed. "Him against me!"

Nick struggled up to his knees, bewilderment in his face.

Michael attacked him again, yelling, "Him against me, goddamnit! I want to see this fucker's brains all over the wall. Him against me!"

The VC were gathered in around the table, watching the two Americans with close, intense interest. Below, even the two remaining South Vietnamese had become fascinated and had taken up positions from which they could observe the proceedings.

Nick had the revolver in his hand. He was trembling. He spun the cylinder, and cocked the gun.

Michael stood up and pounded the table. "This is it, mothers! Now he's going to do it! Watch! You watch!"

Nick stared at the Magnum. His hand shook.

"Look at him!" Michael cried. "See! This is it and he knows it. Last chance to lose your money. There you go, boys! That's it—get those bets down. Watch, now. Here he goes!"

Staring at Michael through wide eyes, Nick put the revolver to his temple, hesitated, shaking, then pulled the trigger.

Click.

Nick choked. He went to put the gun back on the table. It fell from his twitching hand. Michael grabbed it up. He spun the cylinder, cocked, aimed at himself with a shout, and jerked the trigger, clicking out. He threw the gun back on the table with contempt.

"More! Put in more! You guys understand *more?* More bullets!" He held up three fingers. "Three bullets! You understand three?"

The officer pursed his lips and looked at his men. They jabbered and pointed to the gun. The officer nodded. He opened the cylinder, slipped in two more cartridges.

"Terrific!" Michael said.

Nick shook his head disbelievingly.

"You or me!" Michael screamed, jabbing his finger at Nick. "Now we got it! You or me!" He leaned back in his chair and rubbed his hands together. "Now we got ourselves a real game."

Watching Michael carefully, the officer put the gun back on the table and spun it. It stopped, the barrel pointing to Michael.

"Place your bets, motherfuckers!" he said

The guards were swept up in the game. They began to yell.

The officer raised his AK-47 a little and kept his eyes on Michael.

"You jokers think I'm in trouble, right?" Michael sneered at them, picked up the revolver, readied it, aimed it at his head, and snapped the trigger. He clicked out.

He laughed hugely. "No way! Never! Mike is mighty. Mike is strong. Mike is magic. Mike lives long. Lemme hear it from the bench! Come on, motherfuckers, lemme hear it!"

He pushed the gun across to Nick, stabbed his finger at him, and screamed, "Do it!" Then he clasped his hands before him, and smiling ferally, said in a low voice, "I'm gonna will us outta here, Nicky. You got an empty chamber in that gun. Just put that empty chamber in your mind."

Lethargically, as if drugged, Nick lifted the gun and made it ready. He looked at Michael.

"Do it!" Mike said.

Nick clicked out, sagged back in his chair.

The guards betting on him whooped and cheered.

Michael slumped, as if stunned, and screwed up his face with fear.

Nick managed to shove the pistol across to him with a little flair, as if challenging him.

Michael frowned gloomily at the revolver.

The rain had begun anew, beating on the thatched roof.

Breathing deeply, as if mustering his courage, Michael picked up the revolver. "Who's for this asshole?" he said, thumping himself on the chest. "Who's for this asshole?" He looked around at the guards as if they had deserted him.

"Who here is for Michael? he asked. "Michael the Archangel?" There was silence in the hut, broken only by the beating of the rain.

Michael stood. "Who . . . here . . . is for the Angel?" he chanted. "The Angel is mighty! The Angel is strong! The Angel is magic!"

The guards stared in fascination.

"The Angel is mighty! Michael is strong! Michael is magic! Now!"

He whipped up the gun up toward the officer's face. "Die, motherfucker!" He pulled the trigger. The Magnum went off, blowing the back of the man's head out and somersaulting him to the floor.

Nick threw himself out of the chair against the guard beside him. He got his hands on the man's rifle and twisted it savagely, slamming the butt into the guard's jaw.

Michael blasted two more guards. One crashed down over the table, toppling it. The other was driven back against the wall, fell half through, and lay with his trunk on the floor, his upper torso dangling outside.

Nick was firing.

Michael snatched up an AK-47 from one of the fallen guards and opened fire with it, backing to Nick's side.

The remaining guards went down, but two managed to get off short bursts. One shredded the wall over Michael's head. Two slugs from the other caught Nick, spun him around and dumped him.

One of the guards, still alive, was trying to lift his rifle.

Michael stitched him with a half a dozen rounds. He slumped and lay still.

Nick was clutching his belly and groaning. Michael dropped to a knee at his side. "We did it, Nicky!" he said. "We got the motherfuckers! Hang on. You're going to be all right. I'll take care of you."

Nick looked into his eyes.

"I will," Michael said fervently. "I promise."

Chapter 3

Michael dragged Nick out of the hut and down the incline to the side of the wired pilings. He opened the gate.

The two South Vietnamese burst out, shoved him aside, and ran for the jungle.

"Help me!" he yelled after them. "Help me, you sonsabitches!"

The foliage closed up after them, obscuring them from view. He could hear them crashing through the undergrowth.

Nick had fallen unconscious. Michael struggled to get him up over his shoulder, staggered to his feet. He carried Nick down toward the river, the rain beating on them. He came to the pit, unshouldered Nick, and laid him gently on the sand. He stood at the edge of the pit, breathing deeply, and looked down.

Steven's fingers were curled around the grating.

Bloated corpses floated around him. He looked up through the bamboo, eyes aglitter with madness and terror. He was gaunt. His gums were bleeding. He made a strangled animal sound.

Michael rolled the anchor stones away and lifted the grating up, threw it aside. He reached down and pulled Steven out of the muck. Steven howled.

"It's all right," Michael said. "We're going home now. Help me with Nick."

Steven sank down to the sand, hugged himself and whimpered.

Michael went back up to the hut, found a piece of rope, and returned. "Steven," he said, "Steven!"

There was no response. He cut a length from the rope, tied it around Steven's neck, held one end in his hand. He lifted Nick to his shoulder and stumbled down to the edge of the river.

Far downstream, there were muffled explosions, the faint scream of jets, the tiny rattle and pop of small arms fire. A large battle was underway.

Michael lost his grip on Steven's rope. Steven came along anyway, like a following puppy, trailing the rope behind him.

An uprooted tree was drifting down from upstream. Michael waded into the water with Nick.

Steven's voice rasped from behind. "Michael?"

"It's all right, Steven."

Michael was chest-deep now. He floated Nick, supporting him with one arm, and struck out toward the tree.

Steven stopped when the water reached his waist.

"We don't belong here in the jungle, Michael. Are we going home now?"

Michael glanced back over his shoulder. "Yeah, Steven. Come on, follow me."

Steven, great doubt in his eyes, stayed where he was. A huge explosion, much closer than the other sounds of battle, made the earth tremble. "Michael? Michael?"

Michael reached the tree, which was turning lazily in the slow current, and pushed Nick up onto it, spitting water and gasping. The waterlogged tree barely supported Nick's weight. His chin was only inches above the surface. Michael pulled dead branches around Nick, and used the remaining piece of rope to tie him to the tree. He fashioned a slipknot, so he could release Nick quickly. Nick was conscious again. Michael unslung the AK-47 from his back.

"Can you hold this?"

"Yes," Nick said weakly.

Michael went back for Steven.

"We're going swimming, Steven," he said, gentle and reassuring. "Okay?"

He took Steven's hand and led him deeper into the water. Steven balked.

Voices jabbered in Vietnamese. Michael looked back to the shore in panic. A squad of VC had emerged from the jungle and were advancing toward the hut with their weapons at the ready.

Michael grabbed the end of the rope and pulled Steven desperately after him, kicking out toward the tree with all his remaining strength. It was only fifteen or twenty feet, but he was exhausted by the time he reached it. He yanked Steven around to the other side.

Steven was treading water and looking about in frightened confusion.

"Ssshhh, ssshhh, now. It's all right," Michael whispered.

They neared a bend. The current took them looping wide around it, and then the hut and the VC were gone from sight. Michael pressed his forehead to the trees and closed his eyes . . . .

They drifted for half an hour. The rain stopped. Nick was alternately unconscious and awake. His eyes were open now, looking dully at the strange, humplike hills bordering the river, the jagged rocks that were occurring along the shoreline with increasing frequency, the dreamy mist.

Steven looked at nothing, just floated alongside the tree with an empty face. Michael had one arm around Steven's shoulders, the other around a big root close to Nick's head.

The artillery and bombs had fallen silent, but the wind still brought them the sound of sporadic small arms fire from ahead.

"How you doing, Nick?" Michael said.

Nick swallowed with difficulty. "I . . . I don't think I can make it."

"Sure, you can. You can, do you hear me? We're all going to make it. Just hang on."

The tree swung out around a jagged outcropping of rock at a bend. The river narrowed, then funneled into a rock canyon with high walls. Stunted, twisted pines grew along the rim and in crevices on the face. The current quickened. A low, rumbling sound came from somewhere ahead.

Steven jerked his head up. "What's that?"

"Wind," Michael lied. "Just wind."

The tree began to move faster, approaching another bend. Michael scanned the cliff walls.

They went skimming around the bend. The rumbling grew louder.

Michael saw an old suspension footbridge spanning the canyon walls ahead of them, dipping down to within a few feet of the water. There was a young Viet Cong squatting with his rifle at one edge of the bridge, idly watching the boiling water below.

"Nick," Michael hissed. "Nick! You gotta take that bastard out!" He pointed.

Nick blinked, trying to focus his vision. He fumbled with the AK-47.

The guard spotted them suddenly and sprang to his feet. He swung his rifle around, pulled it into his shoulder and fired. A line of slugs chewed up the water half-a-dozen feet to the side of the tree.

Nick fired back. The guard's rifle flew from his hands. He spun and fell onto the slats of the footbridge, broke through and dropped into the water.

The tree struck a submerged rock. The jolt tore the AK-47 from Nick's hands. It disappeared under the water. The tree turned around, and went speeding on.

Michael clamped Steven's hands onto the roots. "Hold on tight!"

As the tree passed beneath the bridge, he lunged upward and managed to grab hold of one of the slats

The bridge swung out to the side, bowing deeply, and water boiled up around Michael. The drag of the current against the tree was enormous. The slat cracked, then tore loose. The bridge snapped back and the tree went hurtling forward. The roar of falling water ahead was deafening.

"Get away from the tree! Get away!" Michael screamed at Steven.

He tugged at the rope around Nick, pulled the slipknot free. He wrapped an arm around Nick, jackknifed his body against the tree, and pushed away.

They were powerless against the current. The tree outstripped them. Fifty feet ahead of them it caught against something for an instant then tore loose, lipped the top of the falls, tilted vertical, seemed to hang suspended a moment, then plunged over.

Michael, Nick, and Steven were carried after it. They went sliding over the edge to drop 30 feet down into a boiling pool.

Michael spun head over heels under water, pulled and tugged by conflicting currents, dazzling points of light dancing in his eyes. He clawed and kicked for the surface, one hand clutching the collar of Nick's shirt. He broke through, coughed out water and gasped, was slammed against a rock, carried over it, and buffeted against another.

His flailing hand caught an outcropping, was scraped and cut, then held, and he managed to pull himself and Nick partly up the big boulder. The water broke forcefully against them. Michael was bleeding from a scalp wound. Nick was unconscious.

"Hold on!" Michael yelled at him. "You gotta hold on."

Steven came rolling by. He managed to catch hold of the rock and pull himself up.

Michael lowered his head and closed his eyes, breathing deeply and painfully. When he looked up he saw Steven staring downstream. He followed the line of Steven's vision. "Oh, Jesus!" he said. "Jesus!"

A hundred yards away, a battered squad of Rangers were lying belly down on a series of narrow sandbars, ineffectually trying to return fire against a larger force of VC that had driven them into the river and now had them pinned down. Three choppers floated overhead, their rotors whipping the river into froth and raising clouds of sand. Fire from the machine guns in their open doors raked the treeline as they tried to maneuver over the trapped Rangers. The sandbars were too narrow to land on, and the choppers were trying to bring their skids down within reach of the Rangers' upstretched hands.

Michael gnawed on his lip, then decided. "We gotta get to 'em! Let loose, Steven. Let the current take you down!"

Steven was paralyzed with fear. His fingers remained tightly clasped around the knobs on the rock. Michael grabbed the free end of the rope that was tied around Steven's neck, tightened his grip on Nick, and threw himself into the water. Steven was jerked off the rock. Michael let loose the rope. He went skimming down the river, trying to fend himself and Nick away from rocks with this free hand. Steven bobbed and rolled in the water a few feet to the side of them.

They were thrown violently up on one of the sandbars. Michael struggled to his feet, hauled Nick erect, and stretched a hand up toward a chopper that edged over to them. He squinted his eyes against the stinging sand blown up by the rotors. Crewmen dropped to the floor of the helicopter, leaned their torsos out, and reached their arms down. They got hold of Nick and hauled him up and in.

The fire from the shoreline intensified. Slugs tore into the fuselage. Michael grabbed one of the skids as the chopper began to rise. He was pulled into the air. Steven dangled kicking from the other skid. The chopper went higher, ten feet, twenty feet. . . . Crewmen were reaching down for them, trying to grab their wrists.

The chopper swung back over the foaming rock-strewn river. Thirty feet up, forty . . . Steven lost his grip. He fell, screaming.

Michael watched him going down. "Steven!" he shouted. Then he let go, and went plunging after him. They disappeared beneath the surface, raising two tall plumes of water . . .

Three hundred yards downstream from the sandbars Michael dragged Steven out of the water onto a mud-flat at the mouth of a creek.

Both of Steven's legs were twisted. A jagged end of bone had torn out through the pants over the right one.

Michael knelt over him, his chest heaving, tears streaming down his cheeks.

"Damn you! God damn you!" he shouted.

Steven's face was lacerated and raw. He opened his eyes. They were flooded with pain, but over that was a lunatic, unwavering trust.

"We don't belong here in the jungle, Michael," he said in a tiny voice. "Are we going home, now?"

Michael nodded dully. "Sure. Sure. Ace. We're going home. We gotta just keep moving."

He raised his eyes and looked at the treeline in despair.

Tall, cloud-wreathed mountains flanked the road, immense and mysterious. The road was a river of fleeing humanity, streaming toward Saigon from the battlegrounds north of the city. They moved in oxcarts, on motorbikes and bicycles, in beat-up old cars of French and American manufacture, but mostly they moved on foot, carrying sacks of possessions tied over their backs, or dragging them in carts and on litters, pulling children by the hand. They walked, slumped and tired and defeated and resigned. Along the roadway were wrecked and disabled vehicles: a burned-out bus, an overturned Volkswagen, troop trucks, a jeep nosed down into the ditch. Above, MEDVAC helicopters were skimming in from the battlefields with pods holding wounded men strapped to their skids.

From the distance came the sound of machine gun fire and the dull *whump* of exploding mortar rounds.

Michael was staggering amid the refugees with Steven on his back, fatigue causing blood to trickle down from his nostrils.

From behind him came the noise of an approaching

tank. Michael stopped and turned. The tank was moving quickly. A bird colonel stood in the open turret hatch. Tired, dirty soldiers clung to the outside of the tank in crowded profusion. Refugees were dodging out of the way.

As the tank neared, Michael lunged into the middle of the road. The tank was almost on top of him before it ground to a wrenching, sliding halt. Michael knelt and eased Steven off his back, laying him gently on the ground. Steven was unconscious.

The colonel pulled himself out of the turret and hopped down, swearing and angry. The tank commander, in a white plastic helmet, got out with him.

Michael pointed to Steven. "Take him along."

The colonel looked at Michael's gaunt, torn face, and his anger abated some. "A little R and R and you'll be standing tall again, son."

Michael reached behind himself, fumbling at the back of his pants.

"Watch it, sir!" the tank commander said.

Michael's hand returned to view holding the Colt .357 Magnum. He leveled it at the colonel's stomach and cocked it.

"Take him along," he repeated.

"Oh, shit!" the colonel said.

Michael gestured with the gun.

"All right, son. We'll take your friend. Stand easy."

Michael watched them load Steven onto the tank.

The tank moved off. As it passed, the colonel stared at Michael. "Fuckin' maniacs!"

Michael watched the tank draw away. He slipped

the Magnum back into his waistband and rejoined the trudging flow of refugees.

"Just keep mcving," he said to himself. "I'll be okay. Just keep moving."

Chapter 4

The bullet wounds healed cleanly and without complication. But they kept Nick for another month after he was physically sound again. They kept him at the Medical Headquarters, on the neuro-psychiatric floor.

Nick walked slowly down the corridor. He was thin and the skin was stretched tightly over his cheeks. Around his neck was a plastic ring, and stapled to that was a colored paper marker. He walked with unfocused eyes, with dreamlike movements.

The corridor was crowded. Wounded men lay on stretchers and gurneys along the walls. Some were propped on chairs. There were others, in gray bathrobes, idle among them, or talking to each other in small cliques.

Nick came to a window. He looked down into the courtyard below. Black body bags were laid out in row after row on the sun-baked concrete. Soldiers were lifting them onto wooden pallets, and other soldiers, driving forklifts, were raising the pallets and driving them over to ranks of waiting trucks, where they were loaded into the holds.

Nick took his wallet from his pants. He opened it to a picture of Linda. He studied the photograph without expression. He returned the wallet to his pocket. He looked down into the courtyard. A tic began to pull at the flesh beneath his eyes.

A hand touched his shoulder. He turned. A doctor with an armful of file folders stood behind him.

"If your name Nikanor Chevotarevich?"

Nick nodded.

"Are you sure?"

Nick nodded again.

"What is that, Russian?"

"No," Nick said dully. "Just American."

The doctor took the paper tag at Nick's neck into his fingers and looked at it. It was marked *N.P.* "How old's this thing?"

Nick shrugged.

"Mother and father's names?"

"Lou and Eva."

The doctor riffled through the files, found the one he was looking for, and opened it. "Their dates of birth?"

The tic became violent. "What the hell difference does that make? They've both been dead for over twenty years!"

The doctor cocked his head, squinted, appraising Nick. "Okay," he said. He fixed another piece of colored paper to the plastic around Nick's neck. "You can go. Get the hell out of here."

He hurried away, looking harassed and behind schedule.

Banks of telephones lined the wall in the telephone center of Saigon's General Headquarters Building. The room was huge, and filled with the voices of servicemen queued up in long lines waiting to call home. Nick, wearing a pair of gray washpants and a red checked shirt, was in one of the lines. He had waited for two hours, and now there was only one man left ahead of him. That man was finishing up his conversation.

Nick took his wallet out. He stared at Linda's picture.

The man before him turned. "Okay, buddy, it's yours now."

Nick put his wallet away. He stepped up to the phone. He looked at it for several moments. Then he turned away from it and walked out of the building into the bright, hot street.

He wandered aimlessly through the afternoon and into the evening. He didn't remember where he had been or what he had seen. He found himself on a narrow, crowded street. The flashing neon lights of bars garishly illuminated both sides of it. Soldiers were walking in groups, in uniform and in civilian dress. Vietnamese of all ages chatted away, offering for sale everything from electric blenders to women. Nick hardly heard them.

In the center of the block, he stopped suddenly, then jumped heedlessly off the sidewalk into the dense traffic of the street. Car horns blared, bicycle and motor scooter drivers shook their fists at him. He weaved and dodged to the other side, sprinted a few paces down the sidewalk, and clapped a hand to the shoulder of a soldier walking ahead of him.

"Michael!"

The G.I. turned and looked at him.

Nick took a step back. "Sorry . . . I . . . I thought you were someone else."

The soldier nodded and walked on.

Nick's shoulders slumped. He looked around, then walked into the Mississippi Soul Bar. The place was crowded, and dimly illuminated by lanterns behind red shades of plastic and paper. Vietnamese girls in bikinis and tight, slit dresses danced with soldiers to deafening acid rock, while on pedestals that flanked the bar, a pair of girls wearing only G-strings wriggled their shoulders, shook their breasts, and gyrated and bumped their hips. Nick made his way to the bar, squinting in the thick tobacco and marijuana smoke.

A pretty bar girl in a tight sweater eyed him, then edged to his side. She leaned over and whispered something into his ear.

He stared at her "What?"

"I show you. Come. You come." She took his hand and led him toward a stairway in a corner. "Not like with girls at home in U.S.A.," she said.

Inexplicably, his eyes filled with tears.

"I give you special, crazy fuck," she said, guiding

him up the stairs and around a corner. "Not like home. Come. You come. I make you crazy."

She brought him into a cramped little room with a single lamp, plastic flowered curtains, and a torn mattress on the floor. There were piles of clothes in one corner, and a night table with a hotplate. Next to the clothes, a baby was asleep in a crib made from a wooden packing crate marked *U.S. ARMY*.

She stopped in the center of the room, faced him, slid one arm around his waist, and cupped his genitals with her other hand.

"What you like to call me now?"

"Linda," he said, as if from a great distance.

She laughed "You call me Linda, just like home."

Nick's hands lifted to the top button of her blouse, fumbled it open, and went feverishly down the line of buttons. He yanked the blouse off, threw it aside. He pulled open the waistband of her slacks, got her down on the mattress and stripped her slacks and panties off. He was on his knees above her, staring. She smiled and opened her arms and legs to him.

He got up abruptly and went to the room's single window, which was cloudy with grime. He looked at the grime. He opened the window. Outside was a dark alley. Dozens of old, leaking air conditioners whirred and stuttered in the night. Soldiers were walking down the alley with girls. A couple of motorcycles passed. An army jeep went roaring by.

Directly across from him was an old Vietnamese man with a thin white beard. He was sitting on a wooden chair against a wire fence that protected the small backyard of a building. Spread out on a blanket before him were several white ceramic elephants. He raised his hand and called to passersby, offering the elephants for sale.

Nick looked back to the girl "Hey!" he shouted. "Hey, elephants. Look at the elephants!" Tears were spilling down his cheeks.

The baby woke up and began to cry. Nick looked at the crib in panic. He bolted out of the room, head-

"Wait!" she cried from the top of the stairs. "First you pay me!"

"I can't be there," Nick said, hurrying down the stairs. "I can't be in a room with a crying baby!"

Chapter 5

It was night. To the north and west of the city, the sky was lit with periodic flashes of fire. The sound of artillery fire came rolling in. Sirens wailed in the distance.

Nick was wandering down a narrow, twisting street near the river. There were no other pedestrians, but there were a fair amount of pedicabs carrying soldiers, alone, and in pairs, to one place or another.

Nick's mind was empty. He was sweating and his face was flushed, but he was racked with chills too, which made him shiver and hug himself.

Tonelessly, over and over, he chanted, "Hey, hey, the wind does blow. Hey, hey, the snow does snow. Hey, hey, the rain does rain. . . ."

The sharp report of a handgun made him spin and crouch, his hands lifting, his eyes flicking about. He saw no one. The shot had come from somewhere within a cluster of wooden buildings across the street, which were protected by a high fence of corrugated metal, their eaves and roofs visible above the fence. He heard cheering and hooting, mostly in Vietnamese.

He stared at the fence and crossed the street slowly. He stood before the gate a moment, then opened it and went in. The houses were dark, except for the last one, which was the closest to the river. A lantern glowed outside the door, and there was dim light visible behind curtains.

Nick moved through the yard. Once it had boasted tended gardens. Though flowers still grew in profusion, they now had to struggle against weeds and high grass. There was an air of decay about the place. He stopped by a stand of bougainvillea, and looked down.

Three corpses were sprawled on top of each other. They were all Vietnamese, and each had a bloody head wound.

A door opened. Two burly Vietnamese men came out, holding a body between them. They carried it over to the bougainvillea and dumped it onto the others. It was an American in civilian clothes, about Nick's age. There was a black-edged hole in the man's right temple. The left side of his head was mutilated. The Vietnamese looked at Nick. They said nothing. They went back into the house.

"You seem . . . disturbed," said a lightly accented voice to the side.

Nick turned. A tall man in a white suit and an open-necked linen shirt was standing beside an Alfa Romeo parked next to a leafy arbor.

After several moments, Nick said, "People inside are doing it for money?"

"Mais certainement. Sometimes a great deal of money. Naturally, I do not practice such civilized risk-taking, myself. I myself do not possess the nerve." He smiled self-deprecatingly. "But I am always . . . how do you say . . . looking out for those things quite rare."

He reached into the Alfa Romeo and extracted a bottle of champagne and a polished silver cup. "Champagne, perhaps?"

Nick shook his head.

"Tch, tch. Don't say no. When a man says *no* to champagne, he says *no* to life." He poured the cup full and gave it to Nick. He inclined his head toward the house. "You have seen this before?"

"Up north." Nick drank from the cup.

"Ah, yes. Of course. Allow me please to introduce myself. I am Julien Grinda. And you are?"

"Nick."

"Nick. *C'est extraordinaire!* I have a second cousin who is called Nicolas, and a nephew Nikolai. So you are, *comme on dit, en famille."*

There was a pistol shot from within the house, followed by yelling and cheering.

"I have to go," Nick said.

"But you must come in."

"No, I—"

"But I insist."

"I have to go, Nick repeated.

Julien smiled. "Of what is there to be afraid after

this war? The war is a joke, a silly thing." He refilled Nick's cup.

Nick emptied it in one large swallow and handed it back. "I'm going home, Ace."

Julien was amused. "To the girl who waits. . . ."

"Yeah."

"Naturellement," Julien said. "I pay my players with American cash. However, should you prefer German marks, or perhaps Swiss francs, this of course can be arranged. Anything can be arranged.

"You got the wrong guy, Ace."

"But you must come in."

"No," Nick said, doubtfully.

"Mon cher ami! There can be no harm in it. I insist!" He took Nick's elbow and guided him toward the house. "After all, it may not quite be *le Grand Hotel,* but it is, nevertheless, even for Saigon, really quite *extraordinaire.* Something you must not miss. That is my hope." He opened the door and made a small bow. "After you."

Nick hesitated, then went in.

Julien took him through a narrow hall that was stacked to the ceiling on both sides with cases of French wine and champagne, cases of American liquor, and boxes of cigarette cartons They went into a room of some size. It was crowded with Vietnamese, a dozen or so Americans, Asians from various countries, and several Europeans. There was low, tense conversation and excited murmuring as men moved through the crowd taking and marking bets. The room was lit by a single 300-watt floodlight that hung from a cord directly above a table. Harshly illuminated under this bulb were two Vietnamese, seated on opposite sides of the table, ceremonious wrapping strips of red cloth around their heads. Several tall, bulky Asians stood around the walls at intervals, watching the spectators with folded arms and impassive faces. Pistols in their belts identified them as house guards.

A slim Chinese man stood at one end of the table, holding a revolver. He announced something to the room in Vietnamese, in another Asian tongue, in French, and then switched to English.

"Gentlemen," he said, "the game is made."

The room went quiet. Spectators pressed in around the table. In the rear, standing stiffly still, as if restraining some sort of pulsing tension, and looking on with detachment, stood Michael.

A clerk chalked the final odds on a slateboard. Bottles and glasses were raised in salute. The Chinese referee held the pistol up for everyone to see, inserted a single cartridge into a chamber, and snapped the cylinder closed.

Nick watched the rigid attention.

"One cartridge," the referee said. "The game to be played to completion. Forfeit automatic after delay of one minute."

He placed the pistol on the table between the two Vietnamese.

Nick left Julien's side. He pushed through the crowd to the table, grabbed one of the players, and threw him out of his chair. He sat down, placed his elbows on the table like a man at a bar about to order a drink, and picked up the pistol.

Michael blinked, jarred from his reverie, shook his

head, and looked again. A choked cry burst from his lips.

Nick spun the cylinder while the spectators gaped, cocked the pistol, and pressed the muzzle to his temple. House guards were bulling through the crowd to the table.

Michael shoved people aside, fighting his way forward. He cried, "Nick, no!"

Nick looked up. He gave Michael a calm, searching look, then he pulled the trigger.

The hammer fell on an empty chamber.

A guard seized Nick and dragged him from the chair.

"No! It's my game, my game!" Nick shouted as they wrestled him out of the room and into the hall.

Another guard grabbed Michael and they struggled together for several moments before Michael could break free. He pushed through the crowd and ran into the hall.

In the courtyard, Nick was on the ground. The guard kicked him in the stomach. Nick grunted, grabbed the man's ankle, and yanked him down. They gained their feet at the same time. Nick caught the Asian under the breastbone with a punch that went deep and knocked the man's wind out, then followed with a blow to the jaw that dropped the man unconscious.

"Nick! Michael cried.

Nick turned and ran for the gate.

"Wait!" Michael shouted. "Nick, come back! Come back!"

He went after Nick. He burst through the gate onto

the street, looked both ways, saw a retreating figure at one end, and raced after it. He tripped over something halfway down the block and went head over heels. He got up, shaken and short of breath. He leaned against a lamppost. He closed his eyes. Then he shook his head. He put his hands in his pockets and began walking slowly down the street.

Julian's Alfa Romeo passed. Julien was driving slowly, searching both sides of the street with his eyes.

Nick slumped back in the rider's seat of Julien's car. He tilted his head, staring up into the sky, which flashed as if with heat lightning, as the bombardment outside the city went on.

"If you are truly brave and lucky," Julien said, "I can make you rich."

Nick turned, but didn't answer. He seemed to look through Julien to something beyond. Julien reached into his breast pocket and withdrew a thick sheaf of American bills. He dropped them into Nick's lap. They were passing an intersection busy with Vietnamese and a few wandering Americans.

Nick picked up the bills and looked at them. He threw them out the window. Shouting broke out behind the car, and Vietnamese rushed to the money, began scuffling and fighting over it.

A monstrous explosion outside the city seared the sky with a high, vivid flash of fire, tinging Nick's and Julien's faces with red. Julien gave Nick a long troubled look. Nick rested his head back and closed his eyes.

* * *

Michael was approaching an intersection in the back of a pedicab. Suddenly the sky lit up with the blast of an enormous explosion outside the city. At the same moment, he spied Julien's Alfa Romeo approaching from the opposite direction. As it passed, he caught sight of Nick, resting in the rider's seat. And then the car was gone.

The intersection was in chaos, with dozens of people battling each other for numerous green bills that were fluttering in the updraft caused by the explosion.

The crowd forced the pedicab to a halt. Michael watched them fighting each other for the money. Tears rolled down his cheeks.

Book Three

HOME

1973

Chapter 1

Dense gray-black smoke billowed up from each of the mill's stacks. The funneling smoke merged into a single cloud high above the mill in the cold winter air of late evening. A wind carried the pall over the town and up the surrounding hillsides, soiling the sky.

Beneath this dirty haze on a partly-wooded knoll covered with soot-darkened snow, Michael and Nick's old trailer was decked out with red paper bells, streamers, and ropes of glittering, shredded aluminum. A huge, hand-lettered banner stretched from a point above the trailer door to the lamppost across the road. It said: *WELCOME HOME MICHAEL.*

Off to the side of the dilapidated trailer sat Michael's old Caddy, crusted with snow and ice, all four tires flat and frozen. Nick's pickup stood rusting beside it. Nosed in behind these were a handful of other, newer cars. Music and laughter rang out from the trailer.

Inside, a press of steelworkers and girls in tight slacks and sweaters were congregated. Axel and John were tapping a new keg of beer. Linda was pacing back and forth anxiously, unable to talk to anyone for more than a few moments, turning again and again to the windows to peer out. Stan had taken up a permanent post at the window with the best view and was keeping a lookout. His dark hair was slicked down; he wore a pair of tailored slacks and a starched floral shirt with big collar tips. He'd put on a few pounds that had rounded his face, but the sharp, predatory planes remained.

Every time a car approached, Stan would jump up and point excitedly and shout, "This is it! This is Michael!"

Everyone would press around, and then when the car passed by, Stan would say, "Not yet. Just hold your water, I'll tell you when!"

Axel hammered the spigot into the new keg and filled up his mug. He raised it. "Three cheers for the red, white, and blue!"

He was answered by a chorus of voices. "Three cheers for the red, white, and blue!"

The taxi began its winding way up the hill. Michael sat in the rear seat, his elbow on the armrest, his chin cupped in his hand, staring out the window at the houses they passed, overcome by a sense of time and distance. He felt as if he were looking at photographs from the past. He was wearing his dress uniform, Ranger's beret cocked aslant on his head, pants creased razor-sharp, small drops of water from melted snow beading on his polished jump boots. He was conscious of the medals and ribbons on his chest. They seemed absurd to him.

His duffel bag and gear were piled on the seat beside him. He fussed with them, poking and shifting them, to distract himself from the melancholy that had suddenly engulfed him.

As they topped the hill, the driver said, "Jesus, will you look at all this."

Michael stared at the festooned trailer. As they drew nearer, he saw figures moving behind the windows.

"That's not it," he said suddenly.

"What? Are you sure? That's not it? You said an old black-and-white trailer. You said off Logan Street, just past Beekman."

"I was wrong," Michael said. "That's not it. Keep going. Make the circle and go back down to the highway."

"Hey, now listen. You said—"

"I'm telling you that's not it! Now keep going."

Michael slouched low in the seat as they passed, raised his hands to the beret, shielding his face.

In the trailer, Stan pointer to an approaching taxi. "This is it! Here he is! Here's Michael!"

The taxi went on by, and Stan's face fell.

Beside him, Axel said, "I thought that was him, too."

Stan was agitated. "Well . . . well, hell, his plane could be late, Axel. I mean, take it easy. I mean, you're driving everyone nuts."

Linda turned away from the window, downcast.

"You okay?" Stan said.

She gave him a small, forced smile.

Stan put an arm around her shoulders. "Nick will be back soon, too. I know Nick. I know he'll be coming back."

"Yes," Linda said, without conviction.

"Nick'll be back soon," Stan said. "Right, Axel?"

"Fuckin' A!"

Michael told the driver to pull into the Starlighter Motel. The driver waited while Michael checked in, then helped him carry his bags into the room. Michael paid him, then stood in the doorway and watched him leave.

He went to his duffel bag without closing the door and took out a bottle with a few inches of whiskey left in it. He returned to the doorway and stood there, looking out at the mill, where fires danced behind the windows, and steam issued from vents in great clouds, and the tall stacks fumed smoke up in the sky. He opened the bottle, tilted his head, and drained the whiskey.

The panic subsided, but the fear remained—the blind, nameless fear.

He closed the door. He stood in the center of the room, looking about. Bland wallpaper. A flimsy bed. A plastic-topped night table. Two chairs covered with aqua vinyl. A plastic plant in a flowerpot. An innocuous framed lithograph on the wall.

He carried a chair over next to the bed and dragged his duffel bag up beside it. He rummaged in the bag, took out an eight-by-ten photo of Steven's and Angela's wedding party that he had put into an aluminum frame he'd bought at the PX in Saigon. He looked at the bridesmaid standing beside Angela; he looked at Linda. He studied the likeness for a long time. He dug in the duffel bag again, and came out with a new bottle. He broke the seal, unscrewed the cap, and dropped the cap on the floor. He propped the photo against a pillow on the bed. He put his feet up on the mattress and settled back into the chair.

He looked at Linda and he drank, with slow, steady swallows.

Dawn came thin and colorless over Clairton. The welcoming banner had been shredded by the wind overnight. What was left of it flapped raggedly in two pieces, one from the trailer, the other from the utility pole. There were only two cars left in back of Michael's Caddy and Nick's pickup—Linda's three-year-old Chevy and a new Camaro. A case of beer stood on the Camaro's roof, dusted with snow that the wind had blown up. The Camaro's engine was running, mist clouding from the exhaust pipe.

Axel, Stan, and John emerged from the trailer. They were bleary-eyed and hung over, and hugging themselves against the cold. Linda came to the door.

Below, in the valley, a steam whistle sounded at the mill.

"Come on, damn it!" Axel yelled to Stan, who was reassuring Linda that Nick would be back any day. "I told you we were going to be late!"

They clambered into the Camaro, Stan behind the wheel. He threw the car into reverse, backed, stepped on the brakes, then started forward with spinning wheels. The case of beer slid from the roof and crashed down, spilling cans. Stan braked. He and Axel jumped out, cursed while they gathered up the cans and tossed them into the back seat, then got back in and went roaring off.

"John," Linda said from the stoop, "do you want me to run you down the hill?"

"No, that's all right. The walk'll sober me up."

She kissed him on the cheek. He gave her a brief hug. "They'll be back," he said.

She nodded. John started down the hill. Linda went back into the trailer.

On a street above the trailer, a little up the rise, partly concealed by trees, stood a solitary figure who had watched the departure. He batted his gloved hands together, stamped his feet. He had been there a long time. He started down toward the trailer.

He knocked on the door, waited, knocked again. The door opened. Linda gasped, stunned. He smiled at her.

She recovered and threw herself into his arms. "Michael! Oh, Michael!" She hugged him fiercely.

When they separated, he looked long into her face. Quietly, he said, "You're more beautiful than I've ever seen you before."

She turned away a moment. Then she said, "I was hoping . . . oh, Michael, I was hoping . . . somehow, that Nick would be with you."

"No. I'm sorry. He isn't."

She went back to his arms. Oh, Michael! Everyone missed you so! Welcome home!"

They released each other. She looked at him searchingly.

"Any word on Nick?" she asked.

"Not a thing. He's AWOL. That's all I know."

They went into the trailer. There were half-eaten cakes, the remains of sandwiches, sixpacks, and empty wine bottles everywhere.

"He's probably just confused," Michael said. "A lot of guys get confused there."

"He never called," Linda said, with a touch of bitterness.

"Maybe he did. Maybe you were at work or out."

Linda forced cheeriness into her voice. "How are you, really?"

He grinned. "How are *you?*"

"Oh, I just go along. You know. I'm still working at the market. It just seems there are a million things to do." Her face became concerned. "Are you sure you're all right? I mean, what about your wounds?"

"Nothing," he said flatly.

"But—"

"It was just some complications. A lot of guys go through it."

Michael studied her face. They stood awkwardly, tensely. Linda turned away, went to the couch, came back with a cable-knit white sweater.

"I made this for Nick. I couldn't remember his exact size, but I think he was the same size as you."

"On the nose."

"Here, take off your coat."

He did, and she hung it on a chair. Linda put the sweater over his head, pulled it down. Her hands jerked as she touched him. The sweater was far too big. It bulked around him and hung well down his thighs.

"It's a little too big," she said, helping him off with it, "but I can fix that. I can— One thing about wool, it's so easy to— Oh, Christ!"

She spun away, wiped a hand angrily across her eyes, stuffed the sweater into the garbage can, and made a little strangled sound.

"How . . . how is the job?" Michael said gently. He could think of nothing else.

She tossed her head. "Oh, great. Great. Just fine. Once or twice we almost had to close. I have to go to work now," she said abruptly. She went to a closet and got her coat out.

"Would you mind if I walked you down the hill?"

She stopped, sighed, and some of the stiffness went from her posture. "You're so funny, Michael. You're always like a gentleman."

Michael looked away, out the window. "Cold," he said. "I'm not used to the cold."

"Do you want some coffee first? I still have some hot. . . ." Her mouth began to quiver. She struggled against it, but tears spilled from her eyes and she began to sob. "I'm so glad you're alive! I'm so happy! I . . . I just don't know what to feel!"

Chapter 2

They walked down the hill to Division Street. A man who had worked with Michael's father stopped them, pumped Michael's hand, and congratulated him on his return. He called over a passing friend.

"Michael here just got back from Vietnam. Say hello to the boy, Harley."

Harley took Michael's hand in both of his and shook it vigorously. "It's terrific what you boys are doin'. We're all in your debt."

Michael said a few polite things, watching Linda as he spoke to the two old men. She was aware of his attention. Unconsciously, she caught her reflection in a store window and primped her hair.

It took Michael a couple of minutes to disengage himself from his well-wishers. Across the street, a coal train rumbled slowly by. He and Linda watched the black, undifferentiated cars roll by. A caboose at the end passed, the rumble of the train faded, and there was a moment of silence, an instant of suspension before the clanging and banging of the mill sounded again.

Michael gave Linda a small kiss on the cheek. She looked at him through wide eyes. He shrugged, took her hand, and they continued down the street. He was uneasy.

"Linda . . . I just want to say how sorry I am about Nick. How . . . I know you loved him and I know it can never be the same. I mean, maybe . . . I don't know if you even want to talk."

She gave his hand a little squeeze, but said nothing.

The supermarket aisles were crowded with crates and boxes. Girls in white smocks were opening them, stamping prices on the cans, and stacking the cans on the shelves. The manager was a harried-looking, round man with fleshy jowls. He was chewing on a cigar and shouting orders to his busy staff.

He broke into a wide smile as Michael and Linda entered, and hurried over to them. He clapped Michael on the back.

"Welcome home, Mike! Goddamn, it's great to see you!"

A number of the girls and bagboys gathered around. They smiled and congratulated Michael, touching his uniform shyly while they welcomed him.

"You did a good job, kid," the manager said. He twisted his head over his shoulder. "Petruccio, gimme a count on those pears!" He turned back to Michael. "I think we got 'em now, you know what I mean? There can't be much fight left in 'em. Here, have a cigar." He stuck one into the breast pocket of Michael's jacket.

A passing stock boy whistled at Linda. "Hi-you, hot lips."

Michael frowned. "They . . . bother you here?"

Linda laughed. "No. Hey, I have to get to work now. Thanks for walking me."

"Listen," Michael said. "Would you mind if I picked you up after work?"

"I'd like that," she said.

In the late afternoon, Michael stood in the mill's huge parking lot, near the changing shed. The first of the day-shift workers were beginning to stream through the doors toward their cars. Michael craned his neck, peering into them.

"Axel!" he yelled. "Hey, Axel!"

Axel, head and shoulders above the rest, looked around, and spotted Michael. He waved and shouted. He grabbed Stan by the arm and pointed. They pushed through the press of workers. Stan reached Michael first, grabbed his hand. Axel hooted, wrapped Michael up in a bear hug, and swung him around.

"Where the hell were you?" Stan said. "We were all set. We had beer, food, everything. Am I right, Axel?"

"Fuckin' A!"

"I got delayed," Michael said.

Axel hugged him again. "Hey, Mike! God damn!"

"Jesus, you must be dying for a shot of real American booze."

Michael couldn't help smiling. He shook his head. "I'm fine. Hey, I'm fine."

"How does it feel to be shot?" Stan asked.

The question hung in the air several moments.

"It doesn't hurt," Michael said.

There was a brief, awkward silence, but everyone seemed relieved that the question had been gotten out of the way.

"Well. come on," Axel said. "Let's go over to John's and get a drink."

They started toward Stan's car.

"How've you guys been?" Michael asked.

"Same old thing," Stan said. "Nothing's changed. I get more ass than a toilet seat and Axel is getting fatter."

Axel snorted. Then he said, "Show him the new gun. Show him the new gun, Stan."

Stan stopped, looked around. He turned to the side, opened his coat, hiked up his sweater and the sweat-shirt under it, and showed Michael a new, nickel-plated .38 Smith & Wesson clipped in a belt holster.

"What the hell is that for?"

"What's it for?" Stan repeated, as if the question made no sense.

"He's a worrier," Axel said.

Michael shook his head. "Hell, let's get that drink."

They got into Stan's car and drove the short distance to John's bar.

It was already crowded. Everyone wanted to shake Michael's hand, squeeze his shoulder, grasp his arm, touch him in some way. They treated him with grave respect and affection. There were no jokes or wisecracks.

John caught sight of him and hurried out from behind the bar, banded his arms around him and hugged him. "Boy! Boy, oh boy! Are you okay, Mike?"

"I'm fine, John."

"Come on in the back. Let's get away from all these clowns. Come on, Axel. Come on, Stan."

John said something to one of his bartenders, then they went into the kitchen. The doors swung shut behind them, muting some of the hubbub from the bar. The bartender came in a moment later with a fresh bottle of Seagram's, a pitcher of beer, and some glasses. He smiled at Mike, then went back out.

"Here we go." John poured the drinks, raised his glass. "Here's to you, Mike!"

"Fuckin' A!" Axel said.

"And here's to the other guys," said Stan.

Somberness settled over them.

"How's Angela taking it?" Michael asked quietly.

"Not so good," John said. "Worse since she talked to him."

"Worse since she talked to who?"

"To Steven."

"To *Steven?* He's alive?"

They exchanged glances.

"You didn't know?" John said in amazement.

Michael stared.

Tears rolled down John's cheeks.

"Hey, John," Axel said uncomfortably.

Stan put his hand on John's shoulder.

"Mike," John said, wiping the tears away, "we don't even know where Steven is. Angela won't tell us."

"What do you mean?"

"She won't talk to anybody. Nobody at all."

Michael paced the kitchen. He stopped at the rear, looked back at them, then turned and went out the door into the alley.

Steven's mother led Michael up the stairs and down a hall to a room at the end. She knocked. There was no answer. She opened the door, gestured for Michael to enter. She looked at him with immeasurable sadness, then nodded, and went back down the hall, leaving him alone.

The room was dim. Angela was sitting in bed with housecoat over her shoulders, her back propped up with pillows. She was looking out the window. It was dusk outside. The glow of the blast furnaces from the nearby mill played across her face. On the floor, surrounding the bed, were a glut of new appliances: a couple of blenders, a television set, a stereo, a steam iron, a popcorn popper, and several others, some of them still in their shipping cartons. Off to the side, a chubby four-year-old boy was playing with a toaster.

Michael looked from Angela to the appliances, many of which he recognized as wedding gifts, then to the boy, then back to Angela again. She was looking at him, but she didn't see him. Her eyes did not blink.

Michael went to the side of the bed. "Angela," he said softly, "I just heard that Steven is alive."

If she heard him, or even knew that he was there, she gave no indication.

"Where is he?" Michael said.

She began to tremble. She picked up a small transistor radio from the night table and turned it on. She continued to stare through Michael. She moved the tuner from station to station. Then she set the radio aside, took up a magazine and a pencil. She wrote a telephone number in cramped, tiny figures. She tore off a little scrap, with the numbers on it, and held her hand out to Michael.

He took it. "Angela?"

She gave him a strange, twisted smile, then snapped her eyes away from him.

Michael leaned and kissed her gently on the forehead. Angela stared out the window. The little boy continued to play, oblivious to everything but the toaster.

Michael left.

Steven's mother showed him out of the house without words. At the door, she said, "Thank you for coming, Michael."

He started back up the hill toward the trailer. His hand was in his pocket, touching the scrap of paper. It was snowing lightly. He went past St. Dimitrus's. A mass was in progress. The choir was singing, the voices a deep, melifluous rumble.

A telephone booth stood on the corner with its door half open, and snow blowing in. Michael hesitated, fingering the scrap of paper. He stopped, closed his eyes, and pulled the collar of his coat tighter against the wind. He opened his eyes, looked at the telephone booth, then went on up the hill.

* * *

Michael sat in the trailer in darkness. He had pulled his old hunting gear into a pile beside the chair. Light from the lamp across the street spilled in through the window, illuminating an end table beside the couch. There was a telephone on the table.

Michael was staring at it. One by one, he cracked the knuckles of his right hand, then worked through those on his left hand.

There was a scuffling noise on the stairs outside the door. Linda came in, her figure visible in silhouette, carrying a bag of groceries. She turned on the lights.

"Michael?" she said.

"Here, Linda."

"I waited for you."

"I'm sorry. I got hung up on something and couldn't come."

"That's all right." She looked at his equipment. "What are you doing?"

"Oh. Nothing. Just getting my stuff together. I'll be going in a minute."

She set the groceries down. "No, don't," she said. "I've got food. I'll make you a real sit-down dinner."

Michael didn't answer. The silence extended itself, grew palpable.

"Michael," Linda said slowly, "why don't we go to bed?"

"What?" His voice was empty.

Linda waited. Then she said, "It's been a long time. Can't we comfort each other?"

Michael lunged up to his feet. "Not *here!* I got to get out of here!"

He swung his pack up on to his back, picked up his rifle and went to the door.

Linda followed him. "Michael, please."

"I'll be . . . I don't know . . . I feel a lot of distance . . . I'm far away . . .I'll see you, I'll see you," he said, and then he was out the door, moving toward the end of the trailer.

He went to the Caddy. He'd called a garage early in the morning. They'd come out, put new tires on, replaced the battery, and got the car going for him. He threw his stuff into the rear seat, got in, and started the car.

Linda came rushing out. "Michael!" she called. "Wait!"

Linda stepped from the shower in the bathroom of Michael's room in the Starlighter Motel. She took a big bath towel from the bar and began to dry herself.

"It seems sort of strange coming to a motel," she said, directing her voice toward the partly open door.

She wiped a clean circle in the condensation of the mirror and looked at herself. She smiled. She felt pretty; she *was* pretty. Her pulse quickened. She was as excited as an adolescent.

"Do you know what I mean, Michael?"

She wrapped the towel around herself and came out of the bathroom. She stopped, her mouth dropping open.

Michael was sprawled atop the spread on the bed, still in his uniform and boots, sleeping deeply.

Linda went to the side of the bed. She looked down at him, her eyes hungry. A small, involuntary moan escaped her lips. She dropped the towel, turned down the spread and covers, and slipped in beside him. She switched off the lamp next to the bed. She folded the spread over him to cover him, then pressed in close to him. She put an arm around him. She stared out the window toward the fires of the mill, dancing in the night.

Chapter 3

The Bowladrome was crowded. Linda was wearing slacks and a sweater. She stood with her feet together, holding the ball in both hands, studying the pins. She took three quick steps forward, the ball swinging back in her right hand, then swung the ball forward and released it.

Michael didn't watch it roll down the alley. He watched Linda. She was trim, lithe, leggy. She was beautiful to watch.

Seven pins went down. Linda turned to smile at Michael. Sitting at the bar, he smiled back. She waited for her ball to return.

At the far end of the bar, Stan was fast-talking a busty redhead, who smiled dazzlingly, but kept shifting her eyes past him to look at Michael. Michael was oblivious to her.

As Linda prepared to roll her ball again, Stan came up to Michael and clapped him on the back.

"Feels good to be back, I'll bet, huh?"

"Great," Michael said, preoccupied with Linda.

Stan nodded toward the redhead. "What do you think?"

Michael glanced over at her. "I don't know, Stanley."

"Is she beautiful?"

Michael took a closer look. "You want a straight answer?"

"Yeah, of course."

"No, she isn't."

"Do you think she looks intelligent?"

"No."

"No?"

Michael shook his head. "No."

"Well . . . neither do I," Stan said.

Michael was amused. "Then what the hell do you see in her?"

"I don't know," Stan said seriously. "That's what I'm trying to find out. Maybe she's good in bed." He called to her, "Hey, honey, you good in bed?"

The girl gave him a smile of pure, amiable imbecility.

A commotion and loud shouting broke out, half a dozen lanes away. Incredibly, Axel was down at the far end of the alley, on his belly, trapped beneath the rim of the automatic pin setter. His legs were thrashing and he was bellowing. John Welch and Linda were hurrying to him. Michael hopped off his stool and ran after them.

John and Linda each grabbed a leg and tried to pull Axel out.

"I got him, I got him," Michael said, replacing Linda at Axel's left leg. "What happened?"

"His ball didn't come back, so he went after it, and the pin setter came down on him."

Stan was crouched, gripping the pin setter with both hands and trying to raise it.

"Axel, you all right?" Michael said.

"Yeah," came the reply. "But I feel like a goddamn mouse in a trap. Get me out of here!"

John began to laugh. Linda giggled. Stan chuckled. It was infectious. Soon Michael was laughing, too.

"Stan," he said, letting go of Axel's leg, "go get the jack out of my trunk."

Stan left, and was back with the jack in less than a minute. He positioned it under the pin setter and pumped the handle. Slowly, the pin setter lifted.

Axel wriggled out backward, clutching his ball triumphantly. "I got the sonofabitch. Ain't nothin' gonna eat *my* ball."

"You all right?" Stan said.

Axel cupped his great belly in one hand, jiggled it a little.

"Fuckin' A!"

"You sure nothing's broken?" John said.

Axel set down the ball, caught Linda under her arms and lifted her high above his head, then set her back down, laughing. "It's not an injured man who can do that, is it?"

"Well, I think we've had enough bowling for one night," Stan said. "What do you guys wanna do?"

"I thought we were going huntin', eh?" said Axel.

"Who's askin' you?" Stan said.

"I was askin' Mike," Axel said. "He's goin'. But no women."

"Yeah, Mike's going," John said. "Right, Mike?"

Michael hesitated, looked at Linda. They held each other's gaze for a moment, then Linda turned and walked off the lane. Michael watched her go.

"Right," he said.

Axel slapped his thigh. "Fuckin' A!"

Stan hopped up and down. "Just like old times! Right, Mike? Am I right?"

"Fuckin' A!" said Michael, and Axel, and John, in unison.

The wind was sweeping across the high ridge, reddening and stinging Michael's cheeks, driving the snow. Dawn was two hours past, but the sky was colorless and dim. The leafless trees were cocooned in silvery ice, and the moaning wind caused branches to creak, fracture lines to appear in the ice.

Michael was following a set of tracks. The few inches of scuffed snow before each depression, the drag mark, told him it was a buck, and a big one: the stride was long, the depressions deep, and the span of the cloven hooves wide.

His eyes moved in alternation from the tracks to the brush and frozen tree trunks ahead. He was breathing easily. Though he was aware of it in some small corner of his mind, he didn't feel the cold. He was intent upon the deer. That was all that existed: the mountain and the deer. And he was the thin connection between them.

A small movement, far ahead and to his left, caught

his attention. He stopped, dead still, and slowly swiveled his head.

The deer was there, at the edge of a grove of snow-decorated hemlock. Its rack was tall and wide. It had a bull neck and heavy shoulders. Here, this high, against the thin colorless sky, it was imperial and majestic, a thing of primal beauty, lord of the mountain. It stared at Michael. Michael remained still, a fixed part of the landscape, but the deer sensed danger anyway. It pawed at the snow and tossed its head up and down. Then it spun and bounded into the hemlocks, disappearing from sight.

Unhurried, confident, Michael turned toward the hemlocks.

Much lower on the mountain, the highway still visible below, Stan was clawing his way awkwardly up a slope on all fours, his rifle slung over his back. He was short-breathed and gasping. Ten yards further up, John and Axel were standing on a broad rock ledge, waiting for him.

"Jesus!" John yelled. "Look! Look!"

He and Axel snapped their rifles up to their shoulders.

The shots came one atop the other, too rapid to count, and echoes came rolling back from the neighboring peaks.

Stan scrambled up the last few feet to the ledge. John and Axel were reloading.

"Well, where is he?" Stan said, gasping for breath.

"You tell us," Axel said.

"What, are you kiddin'? Are you kiddin' me, Axel?

With that many rounds, you shoulda had five deer!" He wheezed. "If I'd'a been where you guys were—"

John said, "Psst! Stan!" He pointed.

An old, graying buck, looking confused by all the gunfire, had stepped out from behind a tall rock.

"Oh, Christ!"

Stan spun and jerked his slung rifle from his back. It went off. "Shit! Shit!" he yelled, bringing it up to his shoulder, working the bolt, and slamming another round into the chamber. He fired, fired again. The shots went ricocheting off the rock. One pinged back and clipped off a branch nearby. Axel and John dove belly down into the snow.

The deer went over the ledge and headed down the slope in a trot.

"You're mine, you bastard, you're mine!" Stan yelled as he went charging down the slope after it, firing.

The trees were thicker here. The wind had picked up. It sounded like the wail of doomed prisoners. Michael had quickened his pace, glancing back every few minutes to see if the buck had circled around and was following him; they did that sometimes, especially the older, wiser ones.

He was close now. He was pushing the buck hard.

Above the wail of the wind, there came a loud, coughing snort.

The buck was visible for an instant, bounding across a break in the trees.

Michael moved effortlessly into a trot.

Axel and John had a deer. They'd flushed and shot it ten minutes after Stan had taken off after the old, mangy buck. It was hanging from a tree limb outside the old shack.

They were inside, drenched in sweat from the effort of hauling the deer to the shack, their jackets unzippered and open. They sat side by side, guzzling happily from beer cans. There were several empties at their feet already.

"Sweet," John said. "Oh, this is sweet!"

Shots exploded nearby, two of them. Then an interlude of silence, then three more shots in rapid succession. John and Axel stood, went outside.

Stan came charging out of the treeline. "I got one! I got one!" he shouted.

His jacket was ripped. Mud and snow caked the barrel of his gun.

"Yahooo!" he screamed. "I got the sonofabitch!"

He missed his footing and came rolling down the embankment, losing his rifle, covering his face and hair with snow.

It was late afternoon. Michael was moving along a line of cliffs that overlooked a frozen lake. The wind was blowing in gusts, driving the snow wildly. Michael was exhausted. His body was rebelling, but he kept it chained, refused to acknowledge its demands. He was on the deer. He was not going to stop until he had it. Nothing else mattered, nothing at all.

The tracks ended.

Michael stopped. He looked around. There was only the line of tracks he had followed, with his own footsteps beside it, nothing ahead of him.

He hunkered down. The wind drove falling snow against his neck, between his cap and the upturned collar of his jacket. It swirled fresh powder from the surface and dumped it in drifts. That was what had happened to the tracks. The wind had drifted snow over them. Michael squatted, thinking about nothing, looking at the last two visible depressions.

The wind swung to the east, gusted. It swung to the west, whipped at his face. Then for a moment, it died. Completely. And there was an unearthly quiet.

The click of a hoof against stone. Michael went quickly to his feet, raising his rifle.

Forty yards ahead, the buck stepped out from behind an outcropping rock. It was moving at a brisk walk away from Michael, unaware of him, picking its feet up high.

Michael sighted in, just behind the shoulder for a heart-lung shot.

The deer stopped. It turned. It went rigid when it saw Michael. Michael shifted the sights a fraction of an inch, centering them on the chest. The deer trembled, too stunned to move.

Michael began squeezing the trigger. Suddenly he raised the rifle barrel. The shot resounded in the clear, high air, and the slug passed harmlessly over the deer's head.

The deer stood an instant longer, as the report went rolling away, then it turned, raised its great head, and broke into an even run.

Michael watched it go. He shouted, "Okay!"

The deer vanished into the brush.

From the neighboring slopes. the faint echo came back to him: *Okay!*

Night had fallen. The Coleman lantern was lit in the old shack. The wind caused it to sway on the rafter from which it hung. John was atop his sleeping bag, snoring. Axel and Stan, well on their way to being drunk, were cleaning their rifles.

Stan finished his, set it aside, then pulled his .38 from its belt clip and began wiping it down with oil.

"What are you doing with that stupid little gun up here?" Axel said.

"In case. Just in case," Stan said belligerently.

"In case? In case of what? In case you stumble on one of your girlfriends suckin' a forest ranger's cock?"

Stan went pale. He cocked the pistol and shoved it out at Axel. "Say that one more time! One fucking more time! Go on, say it!"

Axel sneered. "You're so full of shit you're going to float away, Stanley! That damn thing is empty now."

"Oh, yeah? Yeah?" Stan's face was furious. "Just try it, you prick. Try it!"

The door opened, swirling wind and snow in. Michael stood there. His smile froze on his face, then was replaced by a sudden, savage grimace of anger.

He dropped his rifle, lunged forward, knocked the pistol out of Stan's hand, and slammed him over on his back.

Stan came up to his feet. "Hey!"

Michael moved on him, fist clenching for a blow.

Axel grabbed Michael from behind. "Easy, Mike, easy!"

"What the hell was that for?" Stan said petulantly, retrieving his gun. "Did you think it was really loaded?"

"Gimme that!" Michael grabbed the pistol. He pointed it up to the roof, pulled the trigger.

The shot was loud in the confines of the small cabin. A splinter fell from the roof.

Axel and Stan stood stock-still, their mouths agape.

John snapped up right in his sleeping bag, blinking and looking around in panic. "What was that? What the hell was that?"

Michael lowered the pistol. He turned it over in his hands, looking at it.

"You guys want to play games?" he shouted. "Then I'm going to play your fuckin' game! I'm going to show you how it's really played!"

He flipped the cylinder open, removed all but one cartridge, and closed it. He spun it around.

Stan was chewing his lip. John stared with disbelief.

Michael's hands shook. He grabbed Stan by the front of his shirt and pulled him in, pressed the muzzle to his head.

A sound of paralyzed terror escaped Stan's throat.

Michael pulled the trigger.

The hammer clicked on an empty chamber.

Slowly, Michael released his hold.

Stan gasped air with strangled sobs. He reeled toward Axel, hands outstretched and reaching; then he doubled over, clutching his stomach, and vomited. He collapsed on the floor at Axel's feet, shuddering and sobbing.

Michael lowered the pistol. He walked to the door, opened it, and stepped outside. He listened to the moaning wind. He raised the pistol, cocked his arm back, and flung it as hard as he could, toward the trees, into the blackness and the snow.

Chapter 4

It was evening, getting on toward suppertime. Division Street was mostly empty as Michael pulled the Caddy up in front of the Eagle Supermarket. There were many empty wire shopping carts along the sidewalk, where customers had left them after loading their groceries into their cars. A clerk was gathering them up.

Michael got out and went into the market. A girl closing out the cash registers said, "Linda's in back."

"Thanks."

"How was the hunting?"

"Fine."

"I wondered—" The girl stopped in mid-sentence; Michael was already striding down an aisle toward the rear.

Linda was sitting on the floor, surrounded by open boxes. She was crying quietly.

He touched her shoulder. "Linda . . . what's wrong?"

She turned a tear-streaked face up to him. She shook her head. "I don't know."

"There must be something."

"I'm . . . I'm just so *lonely.*"

Michael was unable to reply. He swallowed deeply, and said, "I have my car outside."

"No." She shook her head again. "Just leave me alone. I'll be fine. Really."

Michael hesitated. Then he nodded, turned, and walked back down the aisle.

He went outside and sat in the car. He slumped down in the seat, leaning his head back, and stared up at the ceiling, trying to think of nothing.

The clerk rounded up the last of the carts, banging them together and wheeling them into the market. The lights began going out. The clerk appeared, buttoning his jacket. Then the checkout girl. They walked down the street together. Another girl came out. Several minutes passed before Linda emerged.

Michael leaned and rapped on the passenger side window. Linda came to the car. He rolled the window down.

"You okay?" he asked.

She nodded. "Did you ever think life would turn out like this?"

"No."

He unlatched the door and swung it open. Linda paused, then she got in quickly and slammed the door shut behind her.

* * *

The trailer was dark, except for the weak illumination that spilled in from the lamp across the street.

Michael was lying naked atop the sheet, his hands behind his head. His mind was empty, and he struggled to keep it that way.

But his body was tense, tumescent, and hungry. There was a thin slick of sweat on his palms and on the soles of his feet.

He heard the bathroom door open, bare feet padding across the living room to the bedroom. Linda was silhouetted against the window for a moment—nude, head inclined, soft hair swinging over her cheeks, modest breasts dipping, gracefully arched back, slender legs. Then she slipped in beside him.

Her hand went to his cheek, cupped it, then slid gently down, her fingertips trailing across his chest. Her mouth came down on his, open and inviting. . . .

Linda was asleep. Michael stood at the window, looking out to the deserted street.

He turned and looked at Linda. She was on her back, head turned to the side, her hair framing it like a dark halo, arms flung out across the pillows. She looked like an angel in a child's story, a soft, lissome, poignantly beautiful angel.

Quietly, so as not to disturb her, Michael gathered up his clothes and put them on. He paused long enough to lean over and brush his lips across Linda's hair. Then he went out of the bedroom, through the living room, opened the door to the night, and eased it shut behind himself. He put his hands in his jacket pockets, hunched his shoulders against the wind, and started down the hill.

The night was cold and blowy, but the sky was clear, and the multitude of stars were tiny points of hard, brittle light above him. His breath misted in the air.

He walked down the hill to the intersection near St. Dimitrius's where the telephone booth stood. He closed the folding door behind him. The light went on over his head. He looked at the phone.

Down the street, a car engine turned over. The car pulled away from the curb. It passed the phone booth. The driver gave him a moment's idle glance, then the car passed by. Michael watched the taillights recede into the night.

He reached into his pocket and withdrew the scrap of paper Angela had given him. He spread it out flat on the metal ledge beneath the phone. He lifted the cold receiver and held it to his ear. He took a dime from his pocket and dropped it into the slot. He hesitated when the dial tone sounded, then put his finger into one of the holes and began to dial.

The recreation room of the VA hospital was bright and cheery, done with bold colors and comfortable, attractive furniture.

A bingo game was in progress. Several dozen men in wheelchairs were clustered around a podium on which a man was calling numbers into a microphone as he pulled them from a bowl. Each new number was met with a chorus of whoops and groans.

A nurse entered the room, carrying one of the little

rectangular slips of paper that were used for telephone messages. Several of the men looked up hopefully.

She passed them by with a conciliatory smile and went directly to a young man whose legs ended in stumps a few inches down from his torso and were covered with the limp folds of his hospital gown. One of his arms was twisted and rigid at his side. He looked at her in confusion, as if she had the wrong person.

"It's for you, Steven," she said.

"Me?"

"Yes."

He stared at the paper. He dropped his bingo card, seized a wheel of his chair, and led himself hurriedly from the room.

He went down the hall to the phone room, breathless and flush-faced. The receiver of one phone dangled down on its cord, waiting. Steven licked his lips. He wheeled himself around in a tight, indecisive circle. Then, abruptly, he directed his chair to the phone and snatched the receiver up.

"Hello?"

"Steven? Steven, it's me, Mike."

"Michael!" Steven furrowed his brow, agitated. "Hey. Hey. Uh . . . how's things?"

"How's things?" Michael said unbelievingly. "Never mind me. How the hell is it with you?"

Steven's eyes darted around the phone room, down to his chair. A desperate, trapped look came over his face.

"Hey," he said. "Great!"

Three men in chairs passed by the door, their wheels whirring.

"What'd you say? I missed that. What's that noise?"

"Wheelchairs," Steve said soberly.

There was a moment of silence. "Jesus. When are you getting out?"

"I'm gonna stay here a while, Mike."

"What for?"

Steven closed his eyes. He summoned up all the enthusiasm he could muster. "The place is great," he said. "It's like a resort. Basketball, bowling. You name it. Even Princess Grace visited us here. It's . . . it's terrific. Just terrific. Look, Mike. I gotta get back. There's a curfew. Hey, thanks for calling."

He moved to place the received back in its cradle. Before it clicked the connection dead, he heard Michael call, *"Steven!"*

He couldn't see through the tears.

The morning was bright. A few scattered, puffy clouds floated in a delicate blue sky. The cab entered the circular driveway to the VA hospital and pulled to a stop before the entrance.

Michael got out first. He was wearing his uniform, beret tilted on his head, polished jump boots reflecting the sunlight like gems. His movements were crisp and precise.

Axel and Stan got out of the rear seat after him, and John emerged from the front seat, next to the driver. Michael's face was set and purposeful. The others looked awkward and uncertain. They followed him into the hospital.

Michael conferred briefly with a nurse at the recreation desk. He thanked her, turned, and headed for the elevators.

The others took seats in the lobby.

Michael went up to the fourth floor. He stopped a nurse. She directed him to a ward room. There were twenty beds in the big room, all neatly made up, ranked in rows of ten along two walls. There were footlockers at the bottom of each bed. Photographs and pictures torn from magazines were taped up on the walls. Someone at the far end was playing an old 45 RPM record on a turntable. Steven was in his chair, reading a paperback book.

He was startled. "Michael," he said. "I don't want to go home." His hands fluttered around the stumps of his legs, as if to conceal them.

"I know," Michael said.

Flustered, Steven said, "Did you go hunting with the guys?"

"Yeah."

"You get one?"

"No."

"*You* didn't get a deer?"

"I tracked one. A big buck. He was a beauty," Michael said gently. "You would have loved him."

Steven looked down to his lap. "Did Angela send you here?"

"No."

"Good."

Michael went to sit down on the footlocker. It was secured with several big padlocks. Michael looked at them curiously.

"Angela keeps sending me socks," Steven said.

Michael touched one of the locks, a massive steel brute.

"Yeah . . . but it's not socks I got in there. Right."

Steven wheeled himself around to the footlocker. Straining, he bent forward and began opening the locks with small keys that hung from a chain he wore around his neck. He raised the locker's lid.

There were at least a dozen small, white, ceramic elephants in the locker. They were stuffed with money. Rolls of money wound with rubber bands were also visible around and beneath the underwear and toilet articles in the locker.

Michael lifted one out. The bills were all hundreds. He looked at Steven.

Steven was bewildered and frightened. Tears brimmed in his eyes.

"One comes every month, Michael, from Saigon. I don't understand! Saigon's going to fall any day now!"

Men in wheelchairs were going in and out of the room. Michael watched them. His shoulders slumped.

"It's Nick," he said in a flat, dead voice.

"How do you know?"

Michael said nothing. He dropped the roll of bills back into the locker, closed the lid, and fastened the locks for Steven.

"That place is gonna be caught in a terrible shit storm," Steven said. "Where is a guy like Nick getting money like this?"

Michael stood. His eyes were on the footlocker, as if it contained something that was at once horrifying and compelling. He snapped his gaze away.

"Oh—cards, maybe," he said. "I'll find him. Don't worry. It's getting late, Steven. I'm going to call Angela. The guys are downstairs. They're going to help me bring you home."

Steven became panicky. "No! I don't fit in, Mike! No!"

"Goddamnit, I am!" Michael said, almost shouting. "I'm gonna do it!"

They held each other's eyes several beats. Then Steven sank back in his chair.

"Do as your heart tells you, Michael."

Michael nodded. He came around, took hold of the chair's handles, and wheeled Steven out of the ward with quick, hard steps.

He marched down the corridor toward the elevators. A nurse came up, demanding to know what was happening. Then another. He ignored them, moving straight ahead, his eyes burning.

Chapter 5

Saigon was about to fall. The war was ending. America was tense, excited, and apprehensive. The military was in chaos. At such moments, a man versed in the systems can get where he wants to go, if he is determined—clipboards with orders can be stolen from harried clerks, forged papers aren't likely to be closely looked at, a fast, authoritative line of bullshit can get you past uncertain and confused noncoms, and bribes, since they're less likely to be discovered, go farther than they usually do.

It took Michael five tiring days of travel in bits and pieces, but at dusk on the fifth day, he was in a jet transport making its final approach to the Saigon airport. Black smoke hung over the field, bodies were strewn about the tarmac, and half a dozen jet fighters were burning. Squads of soldiers were clearing away debris and setting up perimeter lines. Jeeps and trucks sped back and forth. There was a firefight to the west to the field.

Michael stared out the window. It was like seeing the end of the world.

A colonel across the aisle said, "Jesus Christ, they're hitting the goddamn airport now!"

Michael nodded.

"Assholes!" the colonel said.

The pilot had to use a damaged runway in order to stay clear of the firefight, and the landing was rough. As the plane rolled to a halt, the arriving personnel unbuckled their seat belts and moved into the aisle.

The colonel was giving advice to a nervous young major. "And I'll tell you something else," he said. "Don't eat any melons. They use hypodermic needles here to fill 'em up with river water."

The major looked aghast.

They exited the plane and went down the debarkation ladder. A Huey had set down a hundred yards to the side. People were jumping out of it and starting toward the transport. They were Asian and American, both sexes, and all ages. They wore identification tags around their necks, which whipped about in the downdraft of the Huey's rotors. They clutched suitcases and shopping bags, possessions bagged in pillow cases and sacks. Sirens were wailing. A military police jeep mounted with a .50-cabiler machine gun careened up and came to a squealing halt near the steps.

The MP beside the driver stood up in his seat and cupped his hands to his mouth. "Colonel Crispin!" he shouted. "Is there a Colonel Crispin for the embassy?"

"Right here!" called the colonel who'd sat across from Michael. "Come on, Major. Put some hustle in it."

"Excuse me, Colonel." Michael touched the man's elbow, flashed a manila envelope stamped *Secret—Priority*. He'd fished it empty from a wastepaper basket, and stuffed it with a folded sheet of newsprint. "Can I ride along with you?"

"Yeah, sure. Come on. Let's go."

They got into the jeep, which raced them over to the now-empty Huey.

"Quick as you can, guys!" the helicopter pilot shouted to them. "They're stacked up like cordwood back there and we got to move it!"

The chopper lifted off while they were still buckling in. It skimmed over the city, which was marked in several places by fires burning out of control, and here and there by small skirmishes. Sirens wailed. Military and civilian vehicles struggled through the seething streets. Mobs were looting.

Darkness was falling as the helicopter settled down toward the roof of the embassy. Enormous red beacon lights had been set up on each of the four corners. Mobs of people were milling all around the landing pad. The edges of the pad were guarded by a solid ring of MPs armed with submachine guns. IDs were being checked carefully and the refugees directed one by one toward another helicopter, rotors spinning, ready to ferry them over to the airport. Below, the embassy's courtyard was so packed with refugees, that some of them had been pushed into the pool.

A squad of guards rushed the colonel and the major through the people on the roof to a fire stairway.

Michael went with them. Once they were inside, the guards turned back, except for a corporal and one other who led them down the stairs. Men in uniform were rushing about in a near state of panic on the floors they passed, carrying documents and pieces of equipment, shouting at one another.

They reached the ground floor. A huge, red Coca-Cola machine stood at the base of the stairs.

The corporal, who looked sleepless and dazed, said, "Coke machine. If anybody wants one."

"Corporal," Michael said, putting sharpness in his voice. "We—at least I—have to get to the GHQ immediately."

"That's right," the colonel said.

The corporal shook his head, refocusing his eyes. "We can't get any of you off till morning. You'll have to sleep in the lounge. You might as well relax."

In the morning, a vast, hysterical mob of shrieking Vietnamese was pressed up against the barbed wire barricade that stood beyond the main gates. Michael was in a jeep behind the gates, between the driver and a corporal who held a submachine gun and was licking his lips, fidgeting in his seat. The major and the colonel were in the rear seat.

A white-helmeted MP looked from them to his squad, then to the gates. He raised his hands, chopped it down. "Go!"

The MPs threw the gates open and charged toward the barbed-wife barricade, firing with automatic rifles over the heads of the crowd. They opened a smaller, wire-mesh gate in the middle of the barricade, and moved out, firing.

"Hold on to your asses!" the driver called.

He gunned the jeep and they roared out into the mob, horn blaring, the corporal firing bursts into the air. Grudgingly, the mob pulled back, opening a narrow corridor. A man tried to jump on the jeep. He was struck by the fender as the tightmouthed driver kept the accelerator down.

They broke free, went squealing around a corner onto a side street. The city was mad. No sense could be made of it. They passed streets that were utterly calm, serene even, where there were few people or else where people were strolling slowly and happily, and hardly gave them a second glance. Other streets were awash with clamoring refugees jostling and shoving at each other, and others filled with rickshaws, carts, wagons, bicycles, and motorcycles. Now and then rocks were thrown at them, and once someone took a couple of shots at them.

They made it to the old, columned, colonial building next to the river, which was the General Headquarters. The entrance was set in a high chain-link fence topped with three strands of barbed wire. But there was no mob here—since it was not an evacuation point—and the MPs on duty were more relaxed, even to the point of casualness, than were their counterparts back at the embassy. But if the guards were relaxed, the staff was not. Clerks were wheeling out tall, green filing cabinets and loading them onto trucks. Two corporals dashed by carrying armloads of American flags. Other men were hauling out trunks. A squad was trying to wrestle a big combination safe onto a dolly. There were shouts, curses, people rushing back and forth. Papers and documents lay all about the yard and the stairs. Cabinets and pieces of furniture were strewn about.

They got out of the jeep. "I'm looking for General McDowell!" the colonel shouted.

A sergeant running by gave him a look of incredulity. "You got to be kidding!" he said, with a sweep of his arm meant to embrace the whole of the confusion.

Michael slipped away from the jeep. He went out through a personnel portal onto the street. A taxi was pulling up in front of the headquarters. A captain and a lieutenant hopped out, and went through the gate.

Michael signalled the driver. The cab moved up and stopped in front of him. He got in.

He had the driver take him to the Mississippi Soul Bar. The bar was as dark, steamy, and crowded as it had ever been. But the music was louder, the drinking and shouting more riotous, and the go-go girls on the pedestals had dispensed with their G-strings and were gyrating and bumping and grinding with obscene vehemence. It was ending, all of it, and the celebrants were surrendering themselves to orgiastic release.

Michael walked straight through the bar to the kitchen door and went in. He found the wizened, one-eyed old Vietnamese he was looking for, and paid him fifty dollars for a scrap of information and a set of civilian clothes that more or less fit.

* * *

The darkness was broken by a burning building on the corner. The street was as he remembered it, but littered now with corpses. He had to step over the body of a young girl, ten, maybe eleven years old, with a gaping wound in her chest, in order to pass through the gate in the corrugated tin wall. The courtyard was overgrown with high weeds. The bougainvillea were dead. Empty crates lay everywhere. There was a corpse sprawled in the arbor. A loaded truck was pulling away, driven by a Vietnamese. As it disappeared one of the wooden buildings, the white Alfa Romeo that Michael remembered became visible.

Michael stood a moment, then walked to the building nearest the river. It was shuttered and looked empty. He opened the door and surprised Julien Grindal, who was reaching for the latch from within. Julian was wearing nondescript pants and a torn pullover sweater. He had lost weight and was gaunt.

They stared at each other.

"Who the fuck are you?" Julien said, in accented English.

His mouth took on a belligerent cast.

Michael lashed out and slapped him across the face. "Where is the American gambler, Nick?"

Julien stepped back, hand rising to his cheek. *"C'est extraordinaire!"* he said. "Nick?"

"What happened to Nick?"

Julien shifted uneasily. *"Fini."*

Involuntarily, Michael took a step backward. Watching him cautiously, Julien edged past him. He seemed to gain confidence once he was out in the open. He looked at Michael, gave a little snort, went over to his car, and pulled the door open.

"Hold it, Ace!" Michael crossed to him.

"There is nothing here," Julien said angrily. "There is only what you see. You are welcome to all of it."

Michael dug into his pocket, took out a thick roll of bills. "I want a game, Julien!" He began peeling off bills and slapping them down on the hood of the car.

Julien wavered, obviously attracted by the money. "It is too dangerous in these times," he protested.

Michael laid more money down. Julien pursed his lips, but then shook his head. He brought out his car keys.

"Don't try to start that car, Julien."

Julien puffed up his chest. "I am not afraid of you."

"That's fine," Michael said. He put down more money. "But I want to go to a game with the American. The highest stakes."

After a moment, looking hungrily at the bills, Julien nodded.

"How do you know where it is?" Michael said.

"Because I know."

"How?"

"I just know. Leave it at that."

"Well, then, let's go."

"I must take you by river."

"All right."

"Permit me a moment."

Julien returned to the wooden building. Michael followed him. They went into the room in which the game had formerly been played. The table was still there, dried flecks of red on it. There were broken crates lying about, torn cartons of cigarettes littering the floor.

Julien opened a closet door. He changed from his old pants and sweater into his white linen suit. It was still elegant, but the pants were looking a little worn and shiny at the seat.

"For some reason," Julien said as they left, "I've always felt better in a white suit. And formal dress is appropriate to such a contest, no?"

Chapter 6

Julien's boat was a long, narrow craft powered by a small but noisy outboard motor. Michael sat in the front. They made their way slowly upriver. The VC were attacking on the periphery of the city. The fire-balls of rockets lit up the night sky in the distance and muffled explosions came rolling in moments after the flashes of light.

They passed beneath bridges that were filled with people fleeing to no one knew where. The river itself was cluttered with barges and boats and rafts, loaded to the gunwales and wallowing their way downstream.

Michael watched it all with a sense of detachment. For him, it was history already. All he wanted was to find Nick.

After a quarter of an hour, Julien swung his boat out of the main channel, and in toward a half-rotted dock whose front pilings had collapsed, dropping most of the dock into the water, where it bobbed a little below the surface in waves made by passing craft. On the land, at the end of the dock, stood two Esso gasoline pumps whose delivery mechanisms were padlocked shut and wound around with chains. Beyond them was a two-story warehouse surrounded by truck sheds. A mountainous stack of five-gallon cans stood nearby, gleaming in the moonlight.

Julien ran the boat right up onto the dock. He killed the motor, stepped out into the water. The dock swayed beneath his weight. He came around to the front, dragged the boat farther up the dock, and secured it with a rope. Michael got out. The dock dipped deeper. The water came up nearly to his knees.

There was the sound of machinery from the building—stampings, clinkings, bangings.

"A factory," Julien said. "It makes those cans."

They approached. The sounds of production grew louder. There was an entrance door at the ground floor. Next to it stood a wooden stairway that rose up to a second-floor entrance. Dim light shone through chinks and cracks in the upper story, but nothing could be seen in the lower one.

"Wait here," Julien said. He climbed the stairs and knocked on the door.

It was opened almost immediately, then slammed shut in his face.

Julien pounded on the door and shouted something in Chinese. The door opened again and a tall, scar-faced Chinese stepped onto the landing, and rattled off something in a menacing tone. Julien argued with him.

The man glanced down at Michael, said something to Julien in French.

Julien called down, "We must pay to enter."

"All right," Michael said.

"Five thousand American dollars. The world is ending here. Everything is being gathered up."

"Tell him I accept."

Michael went up the stairs and counted out the money into the man's hand.

"He's got the American player?" Michael asked.

Julien translated the question. The Chinese did not answer. He extended his hand again. Michael put another thousand dollars into it. The Chinese spoke to Julien.

Julien said, "He says they have the famous American who has survived twenty-seven games. He also says that giving this information has deprived him of his valuable time, and that you owe him an additional thousand dollars."

Michael slapped the money hard into the man's hand, with stinging force. The Chinese smiled faintly, then opened the door.

They entered a long, high-ceilinged, poorly lit room, encircled by a balcony. The walls were piled high with cartons and boxes of black-market goods. The noise rising from the ground floor was a furious din and the air was filled with smoke. At the far end of the room stood a small table, illuminated by a hooded drop light. In the surrounding shadows, Michael could make out the dark forms of twenty or thirty men. Seated at the table were two young Vietnamese. One of them held a pistol to his head.

The Chinese led Michael and Julien forward. They passed an armed guard, nearly invisible in the gloominess, and a few paces later, another one.

The noise from the floor below was nearly deafening. The men around the table did not attempt to speak. They made their bets with nods and hand signals. The shorter of the two Vietnamese lowered the pistol from his head and passed it to his opponent. The man spun the cylinder, raised the gun, pulled the trigger. He passed the pistol back to the short man. It was an eerie scene; nothing could be heard over the pounding from below.

Several feet from the table, Michael came to a sudden halt. He raised a hand to shield his eyes from the glare of the drop light. Beyond the table stood a gaunt young American who was watching the players dispassionately, and slowly winding a red cloth around his head. It was Nick, hollowed-cheeked, eyes lifeless, his movements slow and dreamlike.

"Nick!" Michael shouted. "Nick, it's me! It's Mike!"

Nick lifted his eyes. He looked at Michael. His face remained empty.

Michael hurried around the table and came close to Nick. "For Christ's sake!" he shouted. "You got no reaction to me?"

Nick looked at him as a bored man might look out the window at falling rain.

"Nick! *Talk* to me!"

Nick looked directly into his eyes, but didn't respond.

A couple of the gamblers glanced their way, but

found nothing of interest, and returned their attention to the game.

"You always told me *I* was crazy!" Michael shouted. "Why are you doing this? What happened to you?"

Nick was blank.

"I didn't come all this way back here for nothing!" Michael said. "This city's going down by the minute. We gotta get out of here now!"

There was a small *pop* behind Michael. Nick's eyes shifted lazily. Michael turned to follow the look.

One of the players was rolling across the floor, the left side of his head a mass of blood and white bone fragments. He stopped and lay still. A guard dragged him into the shadows, righted the chair, retrieved the pistol, and put it back on the table. The referee signalled to Nick. Nick walked toward the table.

Michael went to Julien, bunched up his lapel. "Get me in the game!" he shouted. "I want to play Nick!"

Julien frowned doubtfully.

Michael shook him. "I want to play."

Julien decided, signaled Michael to follow him. They went back around the table to a door at the rear of the room. Julien knocked. The door was opened a crack. Julien said something. Several moments passed, then the door swung wide, and an Asian guard wearing a U.S. .45 automatic in a shoulder holster motioned them in.

A slender, handsome Chinese sat at a table eating a meat-and-vegetable dish with chopsticks. Behind him stood another two bodyguards, one with a pistol in his belt, the other with a sawed-off shotgun slung over his shoulder on a strap. A color television set was playing in a corner, though none of the dialogue could be heard above the noise of the factory.

The Chinese raised his eyebrows at Michael.

Michael came forward, leaned on the table on his hands, and said, "I want to play. I want to play the American. Now!"

"Why?"

Michael dug in his pockets, pulled out all the money he had and put it on the table. "For this!"

The Chinese looked at the money. He beckoned to Julien. Julien stepped up to him and bent his head close. They conferred for several minutes. Then the Chinese waved a hand and returned to his meal.

Julien came back to Michael. "He says you may play."

They went out. A Vietnamese was seated across from Nick. The referee was inserting a cartridge into the cylinder of the gun, holding it up in the light so that all could see.

Julien spoke to him. The referee shrugged. He said something to the Vietnamese. The Vietnamese got out of his chair and stepped away.

Michael sat down. Nick looked at him, and little lines of puzzlement appeared between his eyebrows.

The referee spun the pistol. It pointed to Nick. Nick picked it up and placed the barrel to his head. He looked into Michael's eyes, the corners of his mouth pursing, as if he was trying to remember something.

"Nick!" Michael said, the muscles of his jaw tight. "It's me, Michael. Remember? Michael! Hey, Nick! It's Mike!"

Nick pulled the trigger. The *click* was just faintly

audible. He set the pistol down and pushed it toward Michael.

Michael picked the gun up, spun the cylinder. "Nick. For God's sake! Look at me. It's Mikey. It's Mike!" He aimed the gun at his temple, began to squeeze the trigger. "It's Mike, Nick!" The hammer fell on an empty chamber. He passed the gun back. "Look at me! See who I am!"

Nick prepared the pistol. He raised it. He pressed the muzzle gently against the cloth around his head. The lines of his frown deepened . . . then he broke into a startled grin of recognition.

He said, "One shot, remember? I love you, Mike."

"Nick!" Michael screamed. He lunged across the table, reaching for the gun.

It went off as his fingers touched it. He and Nick crashed down to the floor, the table tipping behind them. They rolled into a high stack of cigarette cartons, which overbalanced, and tumbled down around them.

Michael came up with the gun. It was wet and slippery with blood. A quarter of Nick's head was gone.

"Nick!" he screamed, then fell on the body, clutching it to him.

The huge, gray carrier lay in the water like a toppled skyscraper. Helicopters circled overhead, coming in at rapid intervals. Navy personnel swarmed to each one as it landed, pulled out Vietnamese refugees and American embassy workers and hustled them off to the side for processing while flight crews rolled the choppers to the side of the deck and pushed them over into the water, since there would be no excess space on the carrier.

The deck was chaotic. Michael debarked from a helicopter with a press of mixed Vietnamese and Americans, some of the embassy wives cradling crying children in their arms, and was directed off to the side where an ensign was jotting down names and identification numbers on a clipboard.

He passed a television crew that had its cameras aimed at a thin blonde woman in her mid-thirties who was wearing a shortsleeved bush shirt that flapped in the wind. Her face was strained and tense. She held a microphone and was looking into the cameras.

"This seems to be the last chapter in the history of the American involvement in Viet Nam," she said. "It's also the largest single movement of people in the history of America itself. It is over. It is finished. There is no more." She paused, tossed her head. "This is Hilary Brown, ABC News, aboard the aircraft carrier *U.S.S. Hancock,* in the South China Sea."

Michael closed his eyes. He put a hand to either of his temples, rubbed slowly. He opened his eyes. He looked to starboard, out across the expanse of gray ocean, where the shoreline could dimly be made out. He nodded to himself, and walked over to the ensign.

Chapter 7

The day was cold. The mountains rose up frozen and colorless around Clairton.

At the curb outside of St. Dimitrius's, a hearse was parked, its engine idling, a thin trail of ghostly exhaust issuing from its tail pipe.

Within, the choir reached a crescendo, their voices swelling up in dark triumph, holding, holding, then falling away leaving a lone singer to draw out a final note, to linger, as if reluctant to end, and then fading into silence.

The church doors swung open into the wintry day. Michael, Stan, and John walked with slow steps out the doors, carrying Nick's flag-draped coffin, and down the stairs. Michael and Stan supported the coffin on one side. Tall and powerful, big John Welch handled the other side by himself. Behind them, Axel wheeled Steven out of the church, and eased the chair carefully down the steps one by one. Angela walked beside Steven's chair, holding his hand, her other arm looped around their son.

They loaded the coffin into the hearse, got into their own cars, and followed the hearse out to the cemetery. The wind gusted as they stood around the open grave, raising swirls of snow, trailing long fingers of smoke from the mill's five great stacks across the sky high above them.

The ceremony was brief. The priest finished with the 23rd Psalm: ". . . Thou preparest a table before me in the presence of mine enemies: thou annointest my head with oil; my cup runneth over. Surely goodness and mercy shall follow me all the days of my life: and I will dwell in the house of the Lord for ever. Amen."

Axel pushed Steven up to the side of the grave. The chair wheels mired in the snow-soggy earth, and the others had to help extricate it. Steven leaned forward in his chair. He dropped a single yellow daffodil into the grave. "Good bye, Nick," he said.

Michael, Stan, Axel, and John each held a single flower too. They dropped them in after Steven's.

Michael lifted his eyes from the grave, out over the thin, weathered headstones on the hillside, toward the fire- and steam-marked, smoking and rumbling sprawl of the mill, then up to the leaden sky.

Linda touched his hand. He wound his fingers into hers. They turned away from the grave and began walking back toward their cars.

* * *

The sign on the door of John's bar said *Closed.* He unlocked the door and went in, held it open for the rest to enter. Axel carried Steven into the bar in his arms and sat him down in a chair. Leaving the *Closed* sign in the window, John shut the door and turned the lock. He dragged a big, round table into the center of the room while the others stamped snow off their boots and shrugged tiredly out of their coats. Michael and Stan set up chairs around the table. Linda sat down with Steven. Angela took her little boy off to the bathroom.

Axel sat down at the table. The leg of his chair was broken, and as his bulk settled into it, it tipped precariously. A muted cry broke from his throat. He shook his head angrily, swiped a big hand across his eyes. He cleared his throat.

"I think this one has a broken leg, John," he rasped.

John nodded dully. He brought another chair. "There's coffee already made," he said.

He went into the kitchen and returned with a pot. He set it on the table and stared at it, as if something were wrong and he was trying to determine what. "Cups," he said. "We need cups." He turned back to the kitchen.

"I'll help," Stan said, nearly inaudibly.

The others got up and trooped into the kitchen with them, except for Angela, who remained with Steven. They began loading up with cups.

"We don't want to get too many," John said.

"I can handle some more," Michael said.

"Put some here, Linda," Axel said. "Load me up."

They had a surplus when they returned to the table.

Axel loked around in confusion. "What should we do with them?" he said.

"Put them on the other tables. They'll get used this afternoon. . . . How does everyone like their eggs?"

"What about just scrambled, John?" Linda said.

"All right with everyone?" John asked. "Oh, the toast! I put it on when I got the coffee."

He hurried back into the kitchen. Stan went with him. John pulled out a tray from under the broiler. He'd caught it in time. He stacked the toast on a plate, got some butter, and went back out, leaving Stan, who was standing quietly, looking around, lip trembling.

Linda helped John butter the toast and pass it out. Stan came from the kitchen. His eyes were red.

"Hey," he said. "Maybe we should start with a beer."

"I'll get 'em," Axel said. He went behind the bar to the tap.

"I'm going to get started on the eggs," John said.

"Let me help you," Linda said.

"No, you sit down. Pour the coffee."

Steven was holding his son on his lap, trying to smile.

"Are you okay?" Angela said.

Tightening his mouth, Steven managed to nod.

"It's . . . it's such a gray day," Angela said, unable to voice anything more specific.

Axel brought a tray with glasses of beer to the table. He set them in front of everyone. Michael looked around the table, into their faces, and then at the glasses. Tears welled up in his eyes and rolled down his cheeks. He opened his mouth but couldn't speak.

In the kitchen, John was stirring the eggs on the griddle. His jaw was tight. He was humming. Suddenly he released a long, shuddering sigh. He began to cry, quietly, but with lurches of his broad shoulders. He choked,

"... Stand beside her,
and guide her ...
Da, da, da,
Da, da, da,
Da, da, da ..."

In the bar, everyone sat around the table in silence, listening to him.

Linda raised her face. Softly, she began,

"God bless America,
Land that I love ..."

Michael joined her. "Stand beside her ..."

One by one, the other melded their voices in:

"And guide her
Through the night
With the light from above ..."

John came from the kitchen. He stood in the door, looking at them with astonishment. Then he picked up on the words and came to stand at the table.

"From the mountains ..."

His baritone rose. They sang together, bonding, the intensity rising,

> "To the prairies,
> To the oceans
> White with foam.
> God bless America,
> My home sweet home. . . ."

The song ended. They all shifted uneasily, feeling awkward and confused.

Michael looked around the table. Only Linda met his eyes. He reached out, took one of the glasses of beer and raised it. He smiled at Linda. She smiled back.

"Here's to Nick!" Michael said.

The others looked up. Tentatively, they put their hands around the glasses. Then they raised them, their faces growing stronger, suffused with love for one another.

"Here's to Nick!" they said, in a single voice of affirmation.